CURIOSITIES
GOES TO WAR!

Thirteen tales of heroic deeds and
narrow escapes, astonishing
creatures and esoteric schemes,
cosmic horrors and urban fantasies,
all set against the backdrop of
World War II.

Climb aboard the train, if you dare,
we may not know where or when it
will stop, but we guarantee to
entertain you en route as we travel
across foreign lands, brimming with
adventure, danger, and intrigue.
There will be dragons.

CURIOSITIES

NUMBER SIX

DJ TYRER
ANYA OW
MARK ORR
RON WOLFE
DAWN VOGEL
JD BLACKROSE
LEWIS GERSHOM
ANDREW J. LUCAS
SUZANNE J. WILLIS
MARCAS McCLELLAN
ADRIAN CHAMBERLIN
SEAN PATRICK HAZLETT
MOUNIA LAKEHAL MERIBOUT

EDITED BY
KEVIN FROST & ANDREW McCURDY
2019

Curiosities #6
©2019 by Kevin Frost

Cover composition by Kevin Frost

ISBN-13: 978-1-948396-10-3 (Print on Demand)

TABLE OF CONTENTS

UNCLE ROBIN

When Kevin first mentioned the idea of putting together an issue of Curiosities themed to the Second World War era, we imagined tales reminiscent of a Jakub Różalski painting. Prepared to read about giant, oil-spewing, diesel-belching, war machines, traveling across Northern European farmland, we were surprised to find submissions trending toward urban fantasy and magic realism. As the month progressed, and we debated the shortlist, we knew this was going to be a thick issue, full of powerful stories about an era that remains, even after 75–80 years, ingrained in popular culture.

Many of us reading this are separated from the war by a single degree. Whether it be through a parent, grandparent, aunt or uncle, the war existed in our lives as children but it was just out of reach, like an echo reverberating into the distance. Real but not tangible. For me, as a child, the war consisted of reruns of *Hogan's Heroes,* staying up late with my dad to watch Steve McQueen race motorcycles in *The Great Escape,* or looking at old photos of dashing, young men, wearing proud smiles and crisp uniforms. My Uncle Robin was one of those men. I remember pictures of him in his fine officer's uniform, young and handsome, a graduate of The Royal Naval College in England.

Perhaps it was the uniform, or maybe the hairstyle

associated with our fathers' generation, but in black and white photos, he looks older than his years. My uncle, Lieutenant Robin Blakeney Hayward, was only twenty-four when he joined the *HMCS Athabaskan* as the ship's navigation officer. The *Athabaskan*, commissioned 14 months earlier, was cutting edge at the time, a Tribal-class destroyer with a crew of 255.

In the early morning hours of April 29, 1944, the *Athabaskan* was patrolling with her sister ship, the *HMCS Haida* in support of a British minelaying operation. They were off the coast of France near the mouth of the Morlaix River when the torpedo struck, disabling the ship. The explosion brought the full crew on deck, most of them teenagers.

I can only imagine the adrenaline and crushing sense of reality closing in on each and every one of them, as they stood side by side, searching the cold, black water with the sobering possibility of abandoning ship. They did not have long to consider their options. Ten minutes after the torpedo struck the *Athabaskan's* fate was sealed. Fires caused by the first explosion detonated one of the ship's ammunition magazines, killing and burning many who had been standing close by. With the ship sinking beneath them, the men had no other option but to jump into the water and swim for their lives.

The dawn was now breaking; their sister ship, the *Haida*, had lowered ropes and scramble nets to the water, risking exposure as long as she could dare. All the men swam for it. They were, after all, swimming for their lives. Thirty-eight made it, climbing the nets to safety. But with full daylight exposing them to airstrikes and radar showing the approach of enemy ships, the *Haida* had no other option but to retreat rather than risk the loss of a second ship. A cutter from the *Haida* remained behind, rescuing another six of the most severely injured (in addition to two of *Haida's* crew who'd been washed overboard during the rescue) before it too was chased off.

It would have been around six in the morning when my uncle saw the *Haida* make its retreat. He was one of eighty-three survivors, scattered over a large distance, bobbing up and down in the frigid North Atlantic, clinging to whatever would float. He was alive but 128 of his crew, most of them only a year or two out of high school, either burnt to death or drowned.

It was April and they were floating, in the north Atlantic, watching as friendly rescue diminished in the distance lost to the swell of waves. There was no more doubt. Within hours they would be dead or prisoners of war. Just imagining the cold, the anguish, and the loneliness they must have experienced in those moments puts a lump in my throat.

Uncle Robin was eventually pulled from the water by one of the German patrol ships. I don't know how long he was in the water. By all reports, the German navy treated the prisoners with dignity and respect. That would not last. Once landed, the men were processed, then transferred to *Marlag Und Milag Nord,* a prison complex near the municipality of Westertimke, in Lower Saxony. It was a complex primarily for those serving in the Royal Navy and Merchant Marines. As an officer, my uncle was separated from the men to spend his first month in solitary confinement.

When Uncle Robin was released from solitary confinement he would be one of over three thousand other POWs, awaiting whatever fate the war would bring. The men were given journals by the Red Cross to record their thoughts, concerns, or anything else that entered their minds. Uncle Robin's journal is full, but not with words. Page, after page, is filled with sketches, watercolour paintings, and illustrations drawn by his fellow POWs. Amazing art, some of it war-related, most of it not. Many of them are simply fun, cartoonish, illustrations lampooning the era. It is heartening to see creativity survived captivity.

While preparing to write this foreword, I watched several videos of surviving POWs held in *Marlag und Milag Nord*. From these interviews, I learned that the prisoners performed plays for one another, sang in choirs, taught and learned languages, read extensively, and participated in various team-based sporting events.

From a childhood story told to me by my father, I knew that sports had been a part of the prisoners' fitness routine. Uncle Robin played rugby in the prison compound. He was a good rugby player, having played when he was a cadet back at the Royal Naval College in Dartmouth. I was chatting with my cousin recently who added a little colour-commentary to my uncle's rugby-playing history. While a cadet at the naval college, Uncle Robin would occasionally scrum with Prince Philip, future consort to the British monarch, Queen Elizabeth the Second. They would have lined-up together more often if not for the fact, Uncle Robin was first-string while Prince Philip was second-string.

With the war nearing its end and the allies advancing across Europe, *Marlag und Milag Nord* became dangerously overcrowded due to prison compounds amalgamating as the Germans retreated to remain behind the lines. Before long, it was not just prisoners filling the compound but, in violation of conventions, German soldiers and heavy military equipment. The war, like a glacier, was moving towards them at a slow and steady pace. Food was becoming scarce and, I imagine, tempers short.

On April 2, 1945, almost a year after being torpedoed in the North Atlantic, surviving members of the *HMCS Atha-baskan* were rounded up and marched out of *Marlag und Milag Nord*, along with 3000 other prisoners, the prison guards, several German military units, and all their heavy military equipment.

Uncle Robin was not among them. He had injured his knee a week earlier in a rugby game and was unable to march at a quick enough pace to satisfy the retreating German officers. He was left behind with the other infirmed, a medical staff, and a minimal complement of guards, comprised mostly of old men conscripted from the local community. Those left behind were spared another of war's horrors. The following day, April 3, 1945, the retreating prisoners, German soldiers, and military equipment came under repeated RAF air attacks and sustained many casualties.

For those remaining in the prison complex, the situation, while not so dire, remained grim. *Marlag und Milag Nord* was now a contested area, caught between the front and retreating lines. Guards and prisoners alike dug ditches in case they needed to hunker down and hide. Finally, on April 27, 1945, the remaining prisoners were liberated by the advancing allied forces and my uncle, with decades of life and love ahead of him, came home.

Uncle Robin is gone, as are most of his generation, but their stories and the stories of their time continue to resonate, like ripples spreading outward. The current issue of Curiosities carries some of those ripples to you. So grab your libation of choice and join us for some R&R in the Curiosities Canteen as we serve-up a baker's dozen—fresh war stories, set across nine different countries, hot off the press.

Andrew McCurdy,
Yarmouth, Nova Scotia
July 2019

Suzanne J. Willis

YEAR OF THE TEACUP DRAGON

IT WAS THE YEAR OF THE BLITZ, when air raid sirens sounded throughout London and the nights brought something more terrible than the ordinary monsters of childhood. It was the year that the plum tree began to fruit, and I learned how to preserve the pears and apples from our old trees to use throughout the winter. And in March of that year, among the things that quickly became ordinary, I discovered something that would change me forever.

It was the year of the Teacup Dragon.

It was an early spring day when my mother took me walking through the woods that backed onto our row of houses. Snow lay among the roots of the trees, which were starting to bud under the grey skies. But the day was warm enough and Mum was happy to be out and about, even though she and I had been awake long into the night, waiting for Dad to come home from his homeguard duties. It was always like that in those days—we lay awake waiting for him ever since the day we found out that my older brother, Albert, wouldn't be coming home at all. On the nights we didn't have to run to the shelter, that is.

Dad didn't want us out walking too far from the shelters, but Mum couldn't stand being cooped up, she said, in that way of hers that made Dad silent and raise his eyebrows in response. They had a way of speaking to one another without words, it seemed. Even more so since we got the telegram about Albert. They never mentioned him to me, but sometimes I would hear them whispering, in the way that people do when they're trying to keep something tucked away tight inside, scared to let it loose.

I trailed behind Mum, listening to the birds and trying to catch sight of the first proper greenery of the season. In the verdant shadows off the path, a fiery flash caught my eye. I walked towards the huge oak tree where a cuckoo was hopping about and pecking at the ground, as the green flames flashed. There, at the base of the tree among shards of eggshell lay a tiny dragon, scales the colour of violets—Mum's favourite flower—beating its leathery wings against the cuckoo's attacks, its poisonous fire burning dangerously near the leaf litter and bark. I knew that dragons weren't supposed to exist, that they were something in story books and imagination. But I also knew enough tales about the fae and the strange superstitions that people had to have always known that dragons were possible. I knew enough to trust that it was a real dragon, newborn and fighting for its life.

It looked like the bird was winning, with the dragon's wings so wet that it was unable to fly. With every flame the snow around it melted, making it even harder for the little creature, as the cuckoo dove toward it, beak and claws cruelly sharp.

Dad hated cuckoos—"nasty things," he'd say—so I wasn't too fond of them, either. I ran towards it and flapped my arms, maybe a little hysterically. Squawking, it swiped my head with its wings then flew off into the darkness of the woods.

I crept closer to the dragon, now resting its head between its front paws and breathing heavily, like a dog come in from a long run. I reached out toward it, then stopped as sparks flew out its nostrils.

"I'm not going to hurt you," I said, sitting down and resting my hand palm-up in the mulch to stop it from trembling. The dragon looked at me with a rather suspicious expression, but at least the sparks stopped. It stretched and flapped its damp, viscous wings.

"Cilla?" Mum would worry if I was away from her too long.

"I have to go." Something rustled in the trees, a something that sounded a lot like an angry cuckoo. "Come with me? I don't think you'll be safe here. But I can help you." I reached out my hand a little further, wondering what mum and dad would say if I did bring it home.

The dragon seemed to be sizing me up, then stood, shook itself off and climbed into my palm.

*   *   *

"But Mum, it was my dragon, I'm not fibbing!" Things had not gone so well in the two days since I found the troublesome creature. How could such a tiny thing wreak so much havoc? My little bedroom had not fared much better than our city under attack from the

Germans bombs: the roof of the dollhouse Dad had made me was nibbled and gnawed at the edges, where the dragon's sharp teeth had taken chunks out of the soft wood. Two of my cloth-and-peg dolls were shredded beyond recognition by his curious claws. His most recent unruly behaviour was to fly around the room, just out of my reach, and breathe fire onto my schoolbooks.

Mum stood in the doorway, looking at the smouldering, ruined pages over which I had thrown my cup of tea in a desperate attempt to extinguish the flames.

"For the love of God, Cilla, you expect me to believe that a *lizard* did all this?"

I said nothing, just pursed my lips and looked to the ground, stamping my feet at the injustice. That was the other problem I had—no one actually believed it was a dragon. When I had run to Mum in the woods and opened my hand, he lay there with his wings tucked away and scales gunmetal grey, with nary a flame to be seen. He had since developed the convenient habit of hiding whenever anyone else was about to catch sight of him.

"I don't know where you got the matches or why you would decide to set fire to your schoolbooks, for goodness' sake, but you'll put them in your satchel and take them straight to Miss White's—no, it won't wait until school on Monday—and explain what you've done."

I opened my mouth, but no words came out. She really was so terribly cross with me that she would let me go out by myself, something she hadn't allowed since Albert's telegram. She turned on her heel and left. I began to pack the books into my satchel, brushing away the thought that Albert would have seen my dragon. Even if the dragon had hidden, Albert would have believed me. But I tried not to think about him too much in those days. Everyone, it seemed, had a brother or an uncle or a father who was gone forever and it didn't seem right to dwell too much.

There was a puffing cough from the top of the bookcase. The dragon looked down at me, head cocked to one side and violet scales gleaming in afternoon light. He at least had the good grace to look embarrassed. I buttoned the satchel and held out my hand.

"I don't think it will do much good to leave you here to your own devices," I said.

He spread his wings and glided down, looping twice around my head, then landed in my hand. "Show-off," I muttered, slipping him into my pocket. As I left the house, he began to gently snore. He could, I had to admit to myself, be incredibly charming when he was asleep.

In the wan sunlight, the streets looked as they always had, for the bombs had come close to us, but hadn't yet ravaged our little patch of London. At the end of our street, I turned left and walked up the hill, past the butcher, the seamstresses and the tearooms, where Vera Lynn sung *We'll Meet Again* from the speakers of the radiogram. I stopped for a moment, letting the song wash over me, closing my eyes to the sunlight and dreaming about the cakes that the tearoom used to sell before rationing. My mouth watered and I sighed, opening my eyes. Miss White's bookshop was in the next block, no more than a minute or so's walk. She was a very particular woman who was known to have conniptions if she saw someone leave a book open, face down. I shuddered to think what she would do when she saw the damage the dragon had done to my schoolbooks. Worse still was the thought of what Mum would do to me if I came back without having seen Miss White.

Squaring my shoulders, I walked towards the bookshop.

"Ow!" I wasn't more than half a dozen steps away from Miss White's door when the dragon dug his claws into my leg. Like a cat impatient for food. I opened my pocket and looked in. "That hurt. Watch where you're putting those talons, if you don't mind."

I began walking again. Again, he dug his claws in, this time hard enough to stop me in my tracks. "If you don't stop that," I hissed down at him "I'll leave you here to fend for yourself. And then where would you be?"

But something was wrong. The dragon was whimpering softly, a distressed sound accompanied by wisps of smoke from his flaring nostrils. I couldn't help but feel sorry for him. I sat on a nearby stoop and took him from my pocket. He wouldn't settle, even though I stroked his head and scratched under his chin. This was different to the rascal who had ruined my room and gotten me into trouble—he was genuinely scared.

It frightened me. So much so that I didn't hear the droning until it was loud enough to be its own warning, without the wail of the air raid siren that followed it a few seconds later. From far above, I heard a whistling. The day was in slow motion, as though I was underwater or in a dream. Mothers were running past me, carrying their children or pulling them along by the hand, towards the public air raid shelter. The butcher, his blue and white apron flapping around his ankles, puffed past as well.

I didn't move. I couldn't.

Then there was Miss White, scooping me up in her arms and running, running, as I buried my head in her shoulder. We were a step or two inside the shelter when we felt the tremendous shake and shock as the bombs hit. Miss White gripped my shoulders, tightly, as the ground rumbled again. Then another and another.

The shaking went on for what seemed like the longest time. No one spoke or cried. There was silence and the awful pause of *waiting,* with everyone holding their breath. My stomach knotted as I thought about Mum, then I wriggled in Miss White's arms, anxious to get back to her. But Miss White held me tight. The sirens continued to wail and the shelter smelt musty and stale, like our house did when closed up over a damp winter.

"Crisps?" Old Mr. Potts pulled a few packets from his shopping bag and passed them around, seemingly unperturbed as he sat there in his tin helmet. Some people munched and the other children started to chatter among themselves, but all I could think of was getting back to Mum. Miss White loosened her grip a little and I remembered my dragon, who may very well have saved me with his distress over the impending bombs. I put my hand in my pocket, as much to comfort him as myself. It was empty.

I shook my head as the crisps came my way, trying hard not to fidget in my agitation. I wouldn't think of him under the rubble, or caught in one of the ground-shaking explosions.

The ground stopped shaking and the enormous, catastrophic sounds of dropping bombs ceased, but it was another ten minutes before the all-clear siren sounded. Mr. Potts, his helmet slightly askew, opened the door and I rushed out into the dust and rubble.

What used to be a row of shops was now piles of broken bricks and smouldering ruins. A row of houses in Gloucestershire Lane had met the same fate. The air was smoky, choking. The silence was broken by shouts and a strangled cry from Miss White as she rushed over to where the bookshop once stood, frantically plucking at books that had somehow, miraculously, survived. I stood in my tiny, broken world and wondered why. Somewhere through the smoke, Mum was calling me, over and over. "Cilla? Where's my Cilla?"

She ran up the hill towards me, tears streaking the dust on her cheeks. Until that day, I had never seen her cry. We grabbed one another, then she stood back and felt my head, my arms, my legs and feet. Surprisingly, she laughed aloud, so that other people turned and stared. My mother had a loud, brash laugh and it cut across the stunned whispers and cries that drifted through the air.

"Not a scratch! I sent you out there and I could never, *never* have forgiven myself..."

"I'm alright, Mum. It was Miss White who helped me, her and the—" my voice caught in my throat as I thought of my dragon.

Mum straightened up and, taking my hand, walked over to Miss White and put her arm around her. She lived at the back of that shop and now there was nothing except a few damaged books and a crater where her home used to be. They spoke in soft voices and Miss White sniffled once, twice, then stood tall, smiling grimly.

"Gerry'll no get the best of us," she said. "I'll take you up on your kind offer to stay, but I'll be rebuilding here, mark my words. Is that not right, young Cilla?" She winked at me, clutching the books tight to her chest.

I couldn't imagine how anyone could rebuild from that—it looked as though there had never been any shops there at all—but I couldn't imagine the world always being like this, either. Everyone always tense and waiting for the sirens, then waiting for the bombs that followed. Rationing sugar and tea and the food that could make you feel properly full. Not knowing when—if—the people you loved were coming home again. Not getting the chance to properly love something you had only recently discovered—like a tiny dragon who had saved my life.

But I swallowed my tears and straightened my shoulders, too. I would be like Mum and Miss White, not letting anything get the best of me.

We turned the corner and there was our house, nestled between its neighbours as though to keep out the cold, with not a scratch on it.

* * *

Mum put the kettle on the hob as Miss White helped with the cups and the milk jug.

"And where's your cup, Cilla?"

Only a few hours ago, I'd used it to put out a dragon-fire burning my books. I ran upstairs to retrieve it. My bedroom window was ajar, early spring breezing through it and clearing the last smell of burnt paper from the room. On my bedside table was the cup and saucer, my favourite—white, patterned with yellow flowers.

"Oh!" Inside the cup, curled up as though it had been made for him, was my dragon. He opened his eyes lazily as I smiled at him. "You're a Teacup Dragon!"

Giving him a name seemed to make him properly

mine. Just as this awful day had made me his.

Downstairs the kettle whistled and Mum laughed her brashest best at something Miss White had said. An afternoon that had tea and dragons and a happy Mum spoke of possibility in a world of loss. Of a world that might turn out well, after all.

*   *   *

Once he had claimed the teacup for his very own, my dragon stopped wreaking havoc at home. Quite a sensible dragon, I thought, to choose a teacup as his comfortable spot. Tea is, after all, one of the most comforting things in life. The first thing the neighbours did after the telegram boy delivered the news about Albert was to make Mum and Dad cups of hot, sweet tea. For the shock, they said. And ever since I had been little, Mum always made me a cup of weak, milky tea when she made a pot for herself and Dad.

But while he calmed down at home, the same can't be said for his conduct outside it. Although he never grew any bigger, I could tell that he was growing up, getting older. His skin lost its soft, lizardy texture and his scales became hard, like tiny jewels laid in an old mosaic brooch. When Mum and I went back to the woods—the bluebells and the snowdrops thick on the ground, the violets making Mum smile—I took him with me. Deliberately lagging behind a little, I took him from my pocket and he stretched his wings. They had lost their delicate translucence, their pattern of fine veins, instead becoming tough, substantial. Wings that were made to soar.

The Teacup Dragon snuffed his snout into my hand and I gave him a little prod. He took off, circling into the green canopy above. The sound of his flight followed me. A circle of bright light shafted through the canopy as the dragon burst through it into the sky above. Then a fearsome wind began, squalling through the treetops and nearly knocking us over. Mum looked shocked as leaves twirled around us and birds squawked in their nests, but I knew that it could only be the beating of the Teacup Dragon's wings that would cause such a fuss. I shut my eyes and could almost imagine they were my wings, beating fiercely under the wide sky.

So I began to let him out on some nights, to fly freely and do the sorts of secret things that dragons must do when they are alone. The morning after the first such night, a squeal from Mrs. Grainger next door and the smash of her milk bottles on the front porch interrupted our breakfast. Something small and charred lay beyond her doorstep, still smoking. Mum rushed over to Mrs. Grainger, who was heavily preg-nant and muttering about neighbourhood louts.

"It looks like a cuckoo," Mum said. "Who would do such a thing?"

I knew very well who. I thought about my Teacup Dragon, who made me laugh with his smoky snuffles and sat on my shoulder while I read my books. Who perched on the windowsill next to me when I stared up at the full moon and looked thoughtful when I asked him where its silver path might lead. Whose presence made me feel safe in an unsafe world. But when the charred cuckoos began turning up all over the neighbourhood, I knew then that, as much as I had grown to love him, my Teacup Dragon was vengeful and I couldn't be sure if that was a good thing or not.

* * *

"Do you believe in dragons, Miss White?" I asked over dinner. It was me and Mum and Miss White, as Dad was off on homeguard duties again. We sat around the table with the lamps low and the windows blacked out.

"A pet dragon is Cilla's convenient excuse for things going wrong," Mum said as she passed the potatoes to our guest.

I frowned and opened my mouth to protest.

"Well, now, Cilla," began Miss White, smiling at me and Mum "it just so happens that I do believe in dragons. And faeries—the ones who will offer you poisoned apples or trick you into going under the mountain —and all sorts of creatures that perhaps other grown ups might think of as silly. Why do you ask?"

"You see, I was wondering if, even though a dragon might be tiny, he could also be dangerous?"

Mum narrowed her eyes at me in a *what now?* sort of look, but Miss White laid down her knife and fork, and leaned toward me. "Size is no measure of strength. Some of the world's most powerful, most wicked of men have been small. But whether someone or something is dangerous or not...well, that all comes down to intentions, my girl. This dragon of yours—good or no?"

Mum kept eating, but I knew she was listening. Once, she would have talked to me about my dragon, even if she did see a lizard when she looked at it. But that was before sadness filled her up and left no room for such things.

"I think he's a bit like me, Miss White. I always try to be good, but sometimes things don't work out the way that they're meant to."

"Like life," Mum said softly.

"Just like life," Miss White agreed.

* * *

Miss White and Mum had both gone to bed—I could hear Miss White's soft snores from Albert's old room—but I was awake with my dragon. I was glad that he hadn't flown off through the window when I'd cracked it open for him earlier. Not just because the cuckoos had begun to fray everyone's nerves, but because I missed him when he wasn't there.

"I wonder where you came from," I said to him in the darkness as I cradled the teacup on my lap and scratched his head as he rested his chin on the rim. I heard him yawn, a growling sound, with the sulphurous smell of matches. "Miss White believes in you, you know. And faeries. Maybe you know faeries too?"

He stood on his strong little legs and breathed out green and amber sparks. Slowly he stretched his wings and beat them softly, reminding me of the cabbage moths that had made a home of our fruit trees. The sparks glittered to life, flitting and dancing about, in a waltz-like rhythm. One-two-three, one-two-three... dancing in the darkness as though my very own faeries had been hiding inside his smoky belly all along. I put my forehead close to his and in that quiet moment, it was as though the faerie-glimmers lived inside me, too. Giving me a life beyond the war and a family missing its only son.

A loud knock came at the front door and the embers faded. Bedroom doors opened and footsteps shuffled in the hallway. I poked my head out my door, but was waved away. So I waited until Miss White and Mum had headed downstairs, popped the dragon in the pocket of my dressing gown and followed, watching from the stair landing. When they opened the door, there was Mrs. Grainger, holding her back and groaning. Mum and Miss White helped her inside, and Mum said "Best get the midwife, it's her time." They helped her onto the edge of a chair, rubbing her back and making soothing noises.

Miss White picked up the telephone and dialled, frowning as she listened to the midwife's response to her request.

"Now, would you like to repeat to me why you'll no be coming to birth this bairn?" Miss White's tone was dark. She nodded, then slammed down the phone and turned to Mum.

"Midwife says she won't be coming out tonight seeing as she's just washed her hair."

"She *what?*" puffed Mrs Grainger.

"Shhhh, it'll be fine. It'll be apples, I've birthed two of my own and there's not much that Louise here doesn't know." Mum sounded so sure, but I saw a look pass between her and Miss White. I went to creep back upstairs as the familiar screech of the air-raid siren sounded through the streets.

Mrs. Grainger swore, and Mum called my name. I ran down the stairs as Miss White took her coat of the hook.

"I'll take her to the shelter," she said.

"You'll do no such thing," Mum said. "We can't move poor Edwina here and she'll need us both. Cilla will stay right here in this house with me." She had a look on her face like she did when she first told Dad that she would wear trousers to the village anytime she pleased. Miss White put down her coat and pursed her lips.

Mum smiled at me. "Now, just this once, you can go and sleep in the Morrison shelter in the back room. Go on, now."

The backroom was dark as I crawled through the entrance to the shelter. Its metal top reminded me of a table and the side-mesh was narrow enough to stop anything from raining down on me. At least, I hoped that was the case.

As I hunkered down in the corner, the air raid siren, Mrs. Grainger crying and the darkness all weighed down on me. I took my dragon from my pocket and held him close. He reached up and gently licked my face. I was crying. It was the most alone I had ever felt. The planes were coming for us. Dad was goodness knows where with the homeguard—they were coming for him, too. Perhaps they would get him and not us. Or the other way around. There was already a big hole in our family where Albert used to be, bigger than any bomb crater. The droning got louder and my breath caught in my chest. I didn't think we could stand any more loss. The shelter felt flimsy, insubstantial, unable to stop me being hurt and too far away from the people I loved to help them at all.

My dragon growled and I wished that I could be brave like him, in the face of this danger. "Those planes," I whispered "are coming for us, like the cuckoo that came for you. But there's nothing I can do." He looked at me, a serious look on his scaly face. "Could you..." I thought of the beating of wings above the wooded canopy and the fierceness that lived in my Teacup Dragon's heart. "Would you go out and make us safe?"

Faster than I could move, he glided from my hand toward the back door. As I fumbled with the entrance to the shelter, he lifted the door latch with his snout then flew out into the awful, dangerous night. The moment he disappeared into the darkness, I wished I had never asked that of him. My cries were lost under the siren and the sound of bombs dropping too-nearby.

Although I knew I shouldn't, I crawled over to the door, held it open a crack and peered out, hoping to catch a glimpse of him, to call him back. But there was no sign of him. *Be careful what you wish for,* Mum was always saying to me. I had sent my Teacup Dragon away.

The sky was bright with moonlight and the flashes of anti-aircraft fire. The planes were coming closer. Far-away, bombs whistled menacingly. Soon, they would be dropping on us. Then, against the moonlit sky, an enormous shadow reared, bigger than any plane. It was dragon-shaped and filled the sky, fierce and wondrous. It became solid, scales gleaming dark violet, black, its wing-span dwarfing the moon. It loomed over the planes and I wondered if those pilots knew that they were being hunted. Flashes like gunfire cracked and exploded against the darkness. The shadow-dragon was knocked backward and its left wing was hit by gunfire. But it held its position, beating its wounded wings and hovering like an approaching storm. From the shadow-dragon's mouth, green-black fire, so bright I had to shield my eyes. A roaring wind and heat made me shut the door. Although the sirens kept wailing, the droning noise of the planes had disappeared. I kept watch for my dragon to return. Had he called the monster that had saved us? Or was he the monster, one that I knew lived inside him, fierce and untamed? After what seemed like forever, the all-clear siren sounded and the night was quiet again, as soft grey ash fell from the sky like summer rain.

*   *   *

"Cilla, time to hop up." It was morning and Mum was smiling at me as she shook me awake. Someone must have carried me to my room and tucked me in. Mum seemed happier than I had seen her in a long while and she chattered away. "Mrs. Grainger had her babe last night. She's resting up now, but you can meet the little one later on. Oh, here's your cup, I'll take it downst—" she made a face and put it down again. "Your lizard seems to have made a home in there. He looks a little peaky, to be honest."

I jumped up as Mum left the room. He'd found his way back! My dragon was curled inside the cup, but he didn't look well at all. He was breathing heavily and his left wing was tattered. All the same, he lifted his head and I scratched softly under his chin. I swallowed back my tears as I remembered seeing the planes fire at the shadow-dragon last night, hitting its wing. "Thank you. You were magnificent."

In return he puffed a wisp or two of smoke and nuzzled my wrist, then curled up and slept. I put the cup in his favourite sunny spot on the windowsill and hoped that I could find a way to fix his wing. The sun glittered on his scales, throwing ripples of indigo light onto the window frame and ceiling. Miss White had been right—even something as little as my dragon could hold a skyful of goodness and bravery inside him.

As I walked out into the hallway, the sound of cracking and flames filled the morning. I raced back into my room, Mum and Miss White rushing up the stairs behind me.

"No!"

White and orange flames crackled and spat from the teacup, roaring like a fire in a hearth. The room smelled of burning sage, rosemary, then the freshness of wild mint. As quickly as it had flared, the fire died. I raced over to the windowsill, too shocked to cry.

In the clearing smoke, my yellow-rosed teacup was unharmed. Inside, on a soft bed of ash, lay a pale lavender egg, bigger than a robin's, not quite as big as a chicken's. The egg was warm to the touch. I held it up to the light and the sun shone through the shell. It was like looking through a quick-flowing stream, trying to make out the creatures hiding at the bottom. Like a tiny fish emerging from the shadows, a shape unfurled inside, no bigger than a thumbnail. A turn this way, a glimpse of dragonish snout. That way, a delicately unfurling wing.

Mum and Miss White were whispering behind me, then I felt Mum's hands on my shoulders. "Part of loving something," she said "is knowing when it's time to let go."

I clenched my teeth, wanting to take the egg and run away, hide with it in the woods beyond. It was my fault that he was injured. My fault that he was leaving as suddenly as he came. "Can't I keep him?"

"Dragons are fire-creatures," said Miss White "like the phoenix. Dying by fire and being reborn from the ashes. A new creature recreated from the old. Familiar and unfamiliar at the same time."

I thought I understood, but my chest was heavy and I was lightheaded. "So my Teacup Dragon is gone for good?"

Once, I would have cried. But if he could be brave, so could I. So, instead, I put the egg back in the cup and together with Mum, walked back to the woods. We found a thick patch of violets near a hollow, moss-covered log. I placed the egg carefully inside the log, so it was sheltered from any predators.

"Do you think he will be alright?"

"I think he's a lot like you, dearest. He will be fine."

I tucked moss around the egg, then kissed my fingertips and pressed it to the shell, like Mum did when she said goodnight. Another dragon would hatch in his place and he would do the things he was meant to do, before a magical fire encased him in an egg and he began life all over again. I wondered if he would remember me, in all the lifetimes that he might have, for all the years stretching ahead of him. I wondered if he would remember that he had saved us.

That was the year that Mum and Dad began to speak to me of Albert again, and the year Miss White sold books near the rubble of her ruined shop. A year of ordinary miracles, in which a baby was born in our house in the midst of an air-raid. A year in which I learned about double-edged wishes and that losses walk hand-in-hand with bravery.

It was the year of the Teacup Dragon.

Lewis Gershom

The Fields of Ice

ANJA ENTERED THE BARN, stepped past the cows, and kicked some hay aside to reveal a chain attached to a wooden door set into the ground. She pulled the chain, opened the door, and descended into the inky darkness. Deep underground were two rooms where her family had been living for the past few weeks. This space was once used as a cellar, an inconveniently placed one at that, but the Stanislaws, who owned the barn, converted it into a hideout for refugees when the war came. A shiver went down her spine as she found her husband, Menashe, hunched over some pots, pans, glass tubing, and a small fire, recording calculations on a piece of paper. The only sources of light were his fire and the yellow pallor cast by their single electric light bulb.

"Look at this," she said, plopping down a newspaper next to his equipment.

"Ei, watch where you throw that thing," he said. Without taking his eyes off the bubbling pot, he thrust out his hand at lightning speed to grab the newspaper. "Do you want to cause an accident?"

"Read," she said, her voice almost loud enough to put out the fire.

Menashe picked up the paper but kept his eyes trained on his wife. Sometimes when the light was low, and before Leon returned from collecting the grass for his father's experiments, Anja's face would turn into her mothers', the jowls on her cheeks, the corners of her eyes reaching toward the ground—just as she looked before the SS officer pulled the trigger.

The newspaper's headline read 'German forces advance on Krakow.'

"They'll be here any day now," Menashe said in a low voice. The chemicals in his pot bubbled slowly.

"We are going to have to leave for Russia soon. Tomorrow if possible," Anja said, deadpan.

"And then where?" He asked.

"United States, Canada, Argentina, I don't know," Anja said. "People have made it."

"Do you see how they treat the blacks in those places? What makes you think they'll treat us any better?"

"So, you'd rather die here, buried beneath a barn in a village in the middle of nowhere?"

"Fine," Menashe said. "As soon as the formula is complete."

"There's more," Anja sighed. "Look." She thrust her hand down and pointed to a smaller headline towards the bottom of the page. MORE SYNAGOGUES SURVIVE FIRES.

Menashe glanced at the headline and scribbled

something down in his notebook.

"So?" he said.

"So?" She repeated. "They are going to find you... they are going to find us!" Anja screamed so loud the cows upstairs stamped their hoofs. Bits of dust and dirt fell from the ceiling. "Don't you care about what happens to this family?"

Menashe shot up and Anja was reminded of how her husband could tower over her. His beard, which normally made him look like a stuffed animal, shaped his face into something like a spade when he was angry. Rather than shout he simply stated, "I'm doing this for our family." Anja was never more afraid of her husband than when he was completely calm.

"I'll be right back. It should be ready." Menashe took his bubbling pot off the flame and set it down on the dirt floor to a cool hiss. Five long minutes later, he was back with a squirming, squawking hen.

"Get this over with. Fast," Anja said. "That animal is making too much noise. Arms crossed, she looked around nervously. "And where is Leon? Hasn't he collected enough bison grass by now?"

"The boy is fine," Menashe said, pulling on rubber gloves.

"We've already lost one son who was 'just fine'. I don't want to lose another!"

"Help me give the chicken the serum," was all Menashe had to say.

Scoffing, Anja put on rubber gloves and took a syringe from a box in the corner of the room. It was one of a few belongings from their old life, all of which belonged to Menashe.

"You took an old hen, yes?" Anja asked. With an unsteady hand, she pulled a small amount of blue liquid into the chamber. The glass was freezing cold in her hands.

"Yes," Menashe said.

"Last time the Stanislaws were angry you took a young one."

Menashe sat down on a stool and held the squirming chicken close to his chest. "I promise you, it's an old one." He put his hand on its breast and felt its heart racing just below the downy coat of feathers. Anja knelt down and held out the syringe. Her hand shook as she prepared to inject the liquid.

"Careful, careful," Menashe said. "Don't stick me with that thing. Not yet anyway." Anja pulled back, and put her hands on her hips.

"I thought you said this one would be safe."

"It is, it is," Menashe said in a tone reeking more strongly of bullshit than the barn above them. Anja stood still, refusing to inject the hen. "You said yourself you wanted to do this quickly."

Anja knelt back down. The hen cried out as she pushed the plunger and the blue liquid penetrated its bloodstream. Menashe let go, and the little creature bolted to the other corner of the room. It flapped its wings a few times, but then calmed down and proceeded to peck and prod at the floor. The temperature in the room seemed to have dropped by five degrees. Menashe cast Anja a quick glance which she ignored. She knew what was coming next. Menashe crept to the corner of the room and seized the hen. This time, when he picked it up, the animal did not move or struggle. Its heartbeat was slow.

Menashe held the hen over a small gas burner. Its feathers did not even singe. There was no smell of burning flesh, no squawking, no smoke. He then set the hen directly on the flame. It sat down on the burner as if it was a pleasant heating pad. Eventually, the burner lost oxygen and the flame went out. Anja and Menashe stared at each other, each standing completely still in the near-darkness.

"It worked," Anja said, almost whispering. "It actually worked." Her breath escaped her mouth in short bursts and her mouth turned into a half smile. "I'm sorry for doubting you," she said. "It just seemed —"

"I know," Menashe said before she could finish her sentence. "Don't apologize."

She walked over to hug him. It had been so long since they last did this, Menashe felt like he was holding a stranger. The whole room actually felt warmer as Anja's face pressed against his and when he closed his eyes, he could see the faces of his dead son Leopold, and mother-in-law. They heard footsteps and the door above them creaked. Menashe let go of his wife. Anja dipped into another room and brought back a pair of pistols. Husband and wife crouched at the foot of the staircase where there would be a clear shot in case an unfamiliar face came through.

"It's me, it's me," their son called. "Put your guns down." He struggled down the stairs carrying a bushel of four-foot-tall blades of bison grass, the main ingredient in Menashe's experiment. At sixteen, Leon was beginning to look like a man. He didn't have a beard yet, though he was immensely proud of the thin strands growing from his cheeks as of last year. He had finally matched his father's height, though he may never match his father's width. From his mother, he received his eyes and dark hair. From eight years living in attics, barns, even beneath churches, Leon inherited a steely resolve and a sharp sense for when everything was just about to go wrong.

"You know, no one believes a couple of Yids like you could afford bullets, let alone know how to use them," Leon chided. Before he could set the grass down, Anja rushed over to hug him.

"Leon, look," Menashe said.

"Look at what?" Leon asked.

Menashe pointed to the hen picking away at the floor.

"So?" He said.

"Pick it up. Feel its heartbeat."

Anja stepped back against the wall to take in the whole scene. She watched Leon remove his gloves, scoop the hen into his bare hands, and move his hands over the animal's body trying to find a pulse.

"Oh my god," Leon said. "Did you..."

"Watch," Menashe said, firing up the gas burner with a flick of a match. "Bring it over here." Leon crouched down and held the hen over the fire. When it didn't react, he gasped and dropped the animal. Menashe cut the gas supply and the three of them watched the animal explore the little room.

"Dad," Leon said, pointing. The hen walked over to a stack of books and began to peck. With each peck, the books momentarily glowed a fantastic iridescent blue. A coat of frost swept over the stack, and disappeared moments later.

"Leon, turn the fire back up," Menashe said. Anja passed Menashe a pair of tongs and he carried the books over to where Leon stood taking special care not to let them touch anything else. Menashe held the books above the flame. There was no effect.

"Everything its beak touches resists flame," Anja said.

"Leon, get me a bowl, please," Menashe said, his voice betraying unusual nervousness.

Menashe grabbed a razor blade from off the table, held the hen upside down by its legs, and made a quick, decisive incision across its neck. Feathers floated to the ground. The skin was broken but no blood appeared.

"What's going on?" Leon asked.

"I don't know," Menashe said. "It should be dead by now." Menashe muttered something in Hebrew under his breath which neither Leon nor Anja quite heard. He closed his eyes hard and compressed the hen's whole torso between his hands. When the blood seeped out of the hole in its neck, it came out as a thick sludge. Menashe dropped the bird to the ground.

"Where's my good knife?" He said to no one in particular.

"Menashe, no," Anja said. "You don't know what will happen."

"We can't have this thing just crawling around touching everything."

Menashe turned around, rifled through a box of junk, and pulled out a giant meat cleaver. Anja held her son back .

With each blow, thick purplish liquid flew across the room. As he hacked apart the animal on the floor, the blade left deep indentations in the dirt. He swung and swung, and after a minute the animal was cut down to a pile of bloody feathers. The temperature in the room dropped again. Everything touched by the blood glowed blue with frost for just a second, including parts of Menashe's skin.

Anja and Leon huddled in the corner of the room. Horrified, their knees buckled beneath, each swing of Menashe's cleaver sent them closer to the cellar floor.

He ignited the burner, held out his left hand, and let the flames lick his fingers.

"I can't feel...I can't feel a thing," he laughed. Anja was too unnerved to respond. Next, he took the razorblade from the table. Eyeing the center of his left hand, he took a deep breath, held the blade to his palm and streaked it across his flesh. He fell to the floor screaming as blood gushed from the wound. Leon leaped from his mother's arms, took a towel from the wall and pressed it against his father's hand. Anja saw Menashe and Leon lock eyes. Her husband smiled in between gasps of pain.

"It works, kind of," he panted.

"Dad—," Leon began to say.

"They burned down the last one...and took Leopold with it. Not this time."

"America, Dad. There won't be a next time."

"The grass...tonight, we make more."

Menashe tightened the rag against his hand, now saturated with blood. He turned his back, and returned to work.

*   *   *

Hours later, Anja and Leon sat on a mattress in the adjacent room. The only source of light was a single candle sitting on the floor.

"We're going to have to move again," Leon said. "If what happened last time happens here, the serum is going to seep into the soil and the whole town is going to get cold. Colder than it should be this time of year. Eventually, the Germans will notice a pattern."

"You didn't see the news today, did you?" Anja asked.

Leon shook his head no.

"The Germans arrived at Krakow this week. They'll be here soon enough. We have to leave anyway."

Leon cursed under his breath, something he had only begun to allow himself to do in front of his mother after Hitler was elected.

"Okay," he said, looking around. "There isn't a lot to pack up here."

"Tomorrow we'll head towards Russia. From there, who knows, maybe we'll get lucky."

"Did you talk to dad about it?" Leon asked.

"Yes."

"And?"

"He has agreed to leave."

Mother and son sat in silence until they heard the upstairs door open and close. Anja handed Leon an unloaded gun. He walked into the main room of the cellar, quiet as a shadow.

Anja waited, sitting on the mattress, clutching the gun she did not know how to use close to her chest. She heard Leon fumbling around in the darkness trying to find the lightbulb. Each second that passed felt like an eternity. Finally, Leon reappeared in the doorway.

"Mom," Leon said. "Dad is gone."

"What?" She said in disbelief.

Leon pulled a flashlight from the box of junk.

"I'm going to go look for him."

"Have you lost your mind?" she said. "What if someone sees you?"

Leon rushed over to his mother and held her by the shoulders. *When did he get this tall,* she asked herself, a thought which seemed totally inappropriate, yet completely unavoidable at this moment. She shook her head at her own thoughts.

"I promise, mom, I'll be fine."

Anja held her son close and then let him go. She knew they needed Menashe despite his increasingly erratic behavior. After all, her husband was the one who could speak Russian. With his blue eyes and wavy dusty blond locks, he was the only one of the three who could pass as a Gentile. Not Anja, Leon, nor her dead son Leopold. After Leon left, Anja once more began the process of packing her entire life into a single suitcase.

*   *   *

Leon emerged into the darkness and picked up the old bicycle the Stanislaws kept beside the barn. His shins burned with each pedal stroke as he flew down the dirt road toward the town's twinkling lights. When the road turned to cobblestone, Leon lost control. He skidded to the ground, and just barely avoided smashing his head.

"Shit," Leon said, looking around, anxious to make sure he was neither seen nor heard. As far as anyone knew the Germans hadn't arrived yet. But who really knew the thoughts of people in this town? Who wouldn't phone in a call to an office in Berlin and let them know about some boy with curly hair and a wispy beard sneaking around at night? But then, lying on the ground, his eyes caught what he knew would reveal his father's location—a trail of blood.

The synagogue was an unassuming, boxy white building sitting at the top of a hill with a low, red brick roof, much like the rest of the buildings in town. If you didn't know to look for the faint Magen David above the entrance, you never would have known that a congregation had been meeting weekly here for over four hundred years.

By now, Leon had spent nearly half of his life moving from place to place with his parents. He could just barely remember the synagogue in the town where they lived before the 1930 elections, the bimah, the old Torah the Rabbi read from, its power stronger than magnetism. He remembered the clothes he had to wear, so different and darker than what he wore the rest of the week, not to mention what the others in town wore to their churches. There was the music during celebrations—the melancholy mix of violins, clarinets, and accordions with a beat that weaved, moved from side to side, up and down, never quite where he expected it to land. He remembered how the flames consumed the old synagogue the night his family fled, his mother's unearthly wailing as they ran into the cover of night knowing Leopold was locked inside, burning alive along with the Torah, the pews, and nearly every Jewish person they knew. As he walked inside, all of this came back with surprising clarity, memories buried underground, emerging from beneath melting snow.

The air in the synagogue was already freezing. Leon took out his flashlight and examined the room. He pointed the flashlight at the bimah and the light hit a gaunt, angular face with a thick beard.

"Dad," Leon called out.

"Leon," Menashe said. "What are you doing here?"

"We need to go. Mom said so."

"I'm not going with you to Russia. I'm staying here."

Leon stood speechless in the doorway, not able to believe what he was hearing. Menashe opened the ark and picked up the Torah, his knees unsteady. Leon walked closer to see what his father was about to do.

"You know, kid, I haven't gotten a chance to be up

close with one of these since I was thirteen." He removed the cloak and crown and cast them both aside. He unrolled the Torah slightly, picked up a spray gun, and began to cover it in the serum. "Our suffering is over," Menashe said, adjusting the shafts so he could get to a new section of text. "They will never again control our people." With each coat of the serum, the Torah glowed brighter in the darkness.

Menashe lit a match and held it to the scroll. After half a minute it still didn't burn. Menashe fell to knees, lifted his hands up, and started to laugh, shouting at everyone and no one at the same time. He stood, put his head down and switched to Hebrew, saying words Leon had heard at least once before, but which he did not understand. While Menashe was celebrating, Leon lit the flashlight and shone it over the Torah.

"Dad, I think you should see this."

"Not now, son," Menashe muttered in between breaths. He continued praying in hushed tones.

"Dad, the text...look!"

Menashe stopped speaking and glanced at the Torah. The letters seemed to raise, like they were sitting on top of the sheepskin scroll. When he touched the scroll, they fell away and disintegrated like dust.

"No, no," he said. "This is impossible." He picked up the Torah, placed it on the ground and unrolled it. With each inch the scroll unrolled, the words slid to the ground in a fine powder. Were he not so panicked, Leon would have been impressed that the Torah unrolled thirty feet to the synagogue's door with more to go. Menashe snatched the flashlight from Leon's hand, got down on his knees, and inspected every inch already visible. Not even an outline remained.

"Dad, leave this," Leon pleaded. "If the synagogue

doesn't burn down, the Germans will just knock it down. Then they'll come for us."

Menashe ignored Leon and sat on his knees, trying to find any word that had not been erased. Suddenly, Menashe's head perked up.

"Do you hear that?" He asked.

"Hear what?"

Leon and Menashe got up and looked out the door. They scanned the horizon and saw a small blaze by the Stanislaws' home.

"They've already found us," Menashe muttered.

"Once the barn burns down, they'll find mom in the cellar. It's already been fireproofed," Leon said. With that, father and son took off into the night.

* * *

The Stanislaws' home was burning when Leon and Menashe arrived, but the barn had already been reduced to smoldering rubble. Two SS officers leaned against an unmarked truck and chatted idly. Menashe and Leon hid behind a bush and watched.

"What are we going to do?" Leon asked.

"Your mother should still be okay. If we drink the serum, we can take them out and steal the car."

"I'm not drinking it, dad."

"What do you mean you're not drinking it? What have I spent the last five years doing then?"

"The formula isn't complete. You have no idea what will happen if a human ingests it."

"It's complete."

"That's why the hen's blood thickened? That's why the ink dried up? I'm not doing it."

At that moment, Leon saw one of the SS officers scanning the debris. They walked over, found the secret door, and descended to the cellar.

"Mom," Leon gasped. He wanted to run after them, but Menashe stopped him.

"Wait." Once both of the officers had climbed down, Menashe led Leon to their truck. He got in and then re-emerged with a pair of pistols, handing one to his son. "Now," Menashe said.

As quietly as possible, they climbed down the staircase into the still darkness. Menashe and Leon both overheard the officers saying something in German about scientific equipment. A doorknob clicked and the voices continued. Leon and Menashe hurried down into the main cellar room, their guns drawn. The main room was empty, but the door to the other room in the cellar was open. They heard one of the officers say something, Anja's voice respond, and a single shot ring out. Leon got dizzy and braced himself against the stairs. His father, not missing a beat, took a flask out of his pocket and drained it. As the liquid flowed down his throat, his whole body covered in frost and glowed blue in the darkness. The temperature dropped and the room became so cold that Leon, still in shock from what just happened, began to shake uncontrollably. The officers emerged from the room where Anja was hiding and pointed their flashlights at a young boy lying on the stairs shivering and crying, and a tall, ruggedly built Jew with black holes for eyes.

The officers lifted their weapons and opened fire. Leon's body fell to the ground, motionless. Through closing eyes, Leon watched his father stand still, taking bullet after bullet, staring down the Germans until their clips were emptied. With a look on his face betraying no emotion, Menashe reached down to the bullet lodged in his stomach and removed it as if he were removing a feather from his jacket. The wound oozed a syrupy, purple liquid. Each step toward the officers was more labored than the last, as if weights were attached to his arms and legs. The officers reloaded as Menashe struggled to aim his pistol at them. He squeezed off a shot but missed widely. The officers opened fire once more. Menashe took two more bullets in his chest but did not react. One of the officers lunged at Menashe, knocked him to the ground, and strangled him. When Leon's father was no longer breathing, they both put a couple of bullets in his head for good measure.

Satisfied that the threat was neutralized, the Germans began collecting the lab equipment and taking notes on what they saw. Apart from the lab equipment and the piles of that thick, sweet smelling bison grass, it was mostly junk. Old books with Hebrew lettering, completely meaningless to them. They were about to leave when Leon stirred in the corner of the room. He leapt up, pulled the gun out from his waistband and fired aimlessly until there were no bullets left. When he opened his eyes, the Germans were on the ground, blood seeping all over the room Leon had called home for the past four weeks.

Leon rifled through his parents' belongings, trying to find something to take, but he came up short. No family pictures, no heirlooms, not even their wedding rings. The only things they seemed to own were improvised lab equipment and a few scientific books. Leon decided to take his father's bible, written in Hebrew and Yiddish, the only item in the cellar that seemed to mean anything to his parents.

Before leaving, Leon forced himself to take one last look at his parents' bodies, something he did not have the opportunity to do when Leopold and his grandmother were killed. The gunshots left them unrecognizable. Anja's face was twisted in anguish, her skin a greenish pallor. Most of Menashe's head was gone. If his serum had somehow kept him alive throughout all of this, Leon didn't want to know what it would look like when his father awoke. He wanted to stick around, to properly bury his parents, but he knew there was a more pressing matter at hand. Mourning would have to come later.

Leon took the guns and ammo from the Germans, as well as the keys to their car, said goodbye to his parents' bodies, and headed upstairs. He started the engine, and drove away from the town, silently thanking his father for teaching him to drive just in case an emergency like this would happen. Ten minutes later, Leon hit the brakes, turned around, and drove back. There was something he had left behind.

He parked the car next to the synagogue. The Torah still lay on the ground, absent of all text, unrolled to thirty feet. Struggling to keep his nervous hands from shaking too much, Leon rolled the Torah back up and re-dressed it in its cloak and crown. He had no idea how heavy a Torah actually was, and by the time he reached the car, his arms shook as he struggled to lower it down gently into the trunk.

Back in the car, Leon once again drove off, hoping he was moving towards Russia and not somewhere else. He imagined the Rabbi might wake up tomorrow to open his synagogue only to discover a stolen Torah. But, Leon thought, in a few days everyone who normally gathered here would be carted off to fates unseen. Surely there would be some Rabbi, cantor, or just plain holy person in some faraway place who could rewrite this blank scroll. Until then, it would be Leon's —safe for now in this stolen car, cloaked by night and the snow carried on the ancient, encroaching, wind, soon to transform the countryside into nothing more than empty fields of ice.

JD Blackrose

THE BOOK BURNING

THE LIBRARIAN patted the man on his arm and guided him to a Zane Grey western. The Frenchman spoke English, and he'd come to the American Library in Paris looking for a little break from the war-ravaged world and a way to practice his English. Next to him was a soldier reading a technical manual on refrigerator repair.

Kathryn Dubois kept her smile plastered to her face as she helped Nazi soldiers looking for books to pass the time. Her colleague, Boris Netchaeff, the senior librarian, had been shot in the lung for not raising his hands quickly enough when being arrested. He was alive and in prison, but his fate was a sharp reminder that she couldn't afford to take chances.

But neither could she stand aside.

The front door creaked and Kathryn bit her lip and pulled her shoulders back. Herr Schneider stalked into the library, the sneer on his face almost enough to make her drop her eyes, but she held fast, meeting his gaze. Behind her, she sensed her assistant Madeline shifting to the right to hide in the stacks, such as they were. The library didn't have the resources it should have, but it was all the beleaguered citizens of Paris had.

It was her job to maintain it and keep it open at all costs. Only Countess Clara's relationship with the Vichy Prime Minister, Pierre Laval, made the library's existence even possible. Countess Clara Longworth de Chambrun, the patron of the library, was born in Ohio, but had married Count Adelbert de Chambrun, and thus, had pull. That was the library's saving grace. She didn't advertise her own special, albeit modest talents, which she applied as best she could.

"Herr Schneider, how can I assist you today?" She grimaced as he shot her a disparaging look. No matter how she tried, she'd never get rid of her Marseille accent.

"I'm delivering this list, Madame, and we expect you to follow its directions to the letter. It has come to our attention that this library owns several forbidden books." His upper lip curled in disgust and he almost spit as he said the word "forbidden." He handed her an envelope without looking at her. The envelope was unmarked but the thick linen paper could only come from the Germans.

She opened it, proud that her fingers only trembled slightly. She read the contents, folded the letter, and placed it back inside, taking the moment to gather her thoughts.

"All of these books are forbidden?" she asked. The memo had been crystal clear, but she repeated it just to hear the horrible words out loud. She'd been expecting it, but still, it hurt. Her words also garnered the attention of the patrons in the library who turned to stare.

Appalled as she was by the reason for Herr Schneider's visit, she was relieved he didn't bring soldiers to ransack the library for the books because he might have discovered the basement. She'd spelled the door to creak when Herr Schneider got close so she would have warning of his arrival and a moment of time if required.

"Yes. Prime Minister Laval has approved personally." He sniffed. "I understand many German soldiers come in here to get books."

"Books help the soldiers relax," Kathryn said. "So they can be more alert later."

Herr Schneider dismissed her with a wave of his hand. "Not these books, and we wouldn't want the troops exposed to them, or Paris' citizens for that matter. These books are to be eradicated. Make sure any copies are pulled by tomorrow night. That is all you have to do. I will send an emissary the following morning to gather them." He narrowed his eyes at her. "If that is suitable for you, Madame?" His voice was dry enough to mop off a swimmer.

"What will you do with them?" she asked, although she knew the answer.

"Why, burn them, of course. Good day, Madame." Herr Schneider snapped his heels together, gave her a Nazi salute, and strode out the door.

Madeline tip-toed out of the stacks. "What books are on that list, Madame Dubois?"

"The ones we expected. The ones burned elsewhere." She took a breath. "All Quiet on the Western

Front, The Metamorphosis, Bambi, The Time Machine, The War of the Worlds..." She trailed off and rubbed her eyes.

"Bambi?" said Madeline, her eyes scrunched up. "The story about the baby deer?"

"The very one."

Madeline scanned the list. "The Call of the Wild?"

Kathryn gave a tired nod.

"The Golem by Gustav Meyrink," Madeline whispered. "It's a Jewish story, no wonder they want to burn that one. Do we have a copy?"

"One," said Kathryn.

"Kathryn, what are we going to do?"

Kathryn thought for a moment while a plan formed in her mind. She held up a finger, telling Madeline to wait, and walked behind the checkout desk. She sipped her tepid coffee, mourning the loss of a good café au lait, and sank into her chair.

"Madeline, please collect the books as Herr Schneider requested. We dare not disobey." The girl gave a small, resigned nod of her head and left to do as instructed.

Kathryn walked to her tiny office, a broom closet originally, and lifted the chair onto the desk. She scribbled a note on a scrap of paper and bent to her knees. She crawled under her desk, barely fitting even though she was skinny as a rail and a mere five feet tall. She pushed on a hidden panel and placed the note on a small shelf on the other side. Then she closed the panel and moved in reverse, exiting her office and closing the door with a soft click. She joined Madeline in pulling books, noting that the girl caressed each book with reverence and that fat tears streamed down her cheeks.

As the sky darkened, Kathryn cast a last look at the pile on the table and shook her head, but she gathered her coat to her, picked up a copy of Volk ohne Raum by Hans Grimm, and went outside. She timed it for the busiest time of day, when most people were closing up shop, though there was not much left to sell. It wasn't cold, but she wore a scarf on the outside of the coat and walked at a sedate pace, as if she was simply enjoying the clear evening.

A man who also wore a coat and a scarf passed her on the street and brushed her arm. The book dropped to the ground.

"Oh, I am so sorry," said the man, as he retrieved the book from the concrete. "Are you alright? Did I hurt you?"

"I'm fine," Kathryn replied, placing her hands in her coat pockets. "Please don't worry about it."

"I apologize again. I must remember to look where I'm going."

When they parted, he held the book, and she hurried home.

* * *

She took a different route in the morning and stopped at a small grocery that still had some meager supplies.

"Madame Dubois. Good morning!" said the gray-haired proprietor. "The usual coffee?"

"Yes, please. And a Danish."

The man handed her the hot cup and a paper bag containing a stale Danish and a book.

She opened the library with her normal efficiency, but if anyone was watching, they would have noticed that she whispered a few words under her breath while making a warding sign with her right hand. The squeak was on.

She removed the book, a dog-eared copy of Les Misérables, from the paper bag and opened it to page forty-two, marked by an old postcard from Florida being used as a bookmark. Written on the back of the card was a message saying, "Yes, it is as sunny as you think! You would enjoy it."

The only word that mattered was the word "Yes," so Kathryn removed the postcard, tore it into pieces, and threw them in the trash, returning the book to the stacks.

She'd asked Madeline to stay home that day, telling the sensitive girl that didn't need to witness a book burning. Patrons streamed in and out all day and she helped each one with a smile, but her stomach churned with anxiety. She understood why they came. Books provided a relief from the fear and hunger.

Books were precious, and she was about to help burn a whole stack of them.

She took a small break in her office and swallowed the hard Danish she'd saved from that morning. Her stomach growled.

"Shut up, tummy. We'll get food *tonight*."

She left her office and went back to work.

Just before the library was to close, the door creaked and Kathryn closed her eyes to prepare herself.

"Are the books ready?" Herr Schneider's voice boomed through the mostly empty room. The few patrons left scurried out the door as quickly as they could, never noticing that the door moved silently on its hinges when they opened it.

"Yes, Herr Schneider. I've piled them there." Kathryn pointed to a table straining under the weight of dozens of books. He walked over to them and examined the spines.

"No copies of that perversion of literature, The Golem?"

"No, sir. We don't own any."

"I thought there would be more. I was told that you had a copy of The Sun Also Rises." He turned to her, lifting an eyebrow.

"No, sir. You're welcome to look through the stacks. You won't find it here. We may have had it once but, no longer. Probably burned already."

"Hum. For your sake, I hope what you say is true."

Giving her one last hard look, he snapped his fingers and two soldiers rolled in a wheelbarrow and shifted the books into it. It took them two trips.

The Nazis had decided to burn the books in the street in a public display of might. Kathryn held still, chin up as they poured gasoline on top of the books. People gathered to stare at the spectacle and no one tried to stop the SS officers. Everyone watched, arms crossed tight over their chests, as the soldiers laughed and pulled cigars from their breast pockets.

Herr Schneider, smiling broadly, gave one of the officers a signal and the man took a lit torch to the pile. The fire caught slowly but eventually it crawled over the hardbacks and paperbacks and the flames rose in the growing dark.

"Look at them go up like matchsticks," one of the SS soldiers said, snickering. "They burn like toilet paper."

The soldiers laughed like they could not get enough and several stepped forward to light their cigars in the blaze.

Kathryn stepped back two paces, so she was out of sight but could still see the bonfire. She took a deep breath and held both hands up in the air, moving them in a complex pattern while singing in a soft rhythm, repeating the pattern three times.

As she finished the last round, the bonfire roared to life, flames shooting into the sky in arcs of angry red and yellow. Sparks snapped at the bystanders as if the fire itself was offended at being forced to do this job. The conflagration caught the Nazis by surprise and those that were standing too close caught on fire. They screamed in pain while everyone else ran for their lives.

In the back of the library, a man wore a coat with a scarf. As soon as he saw the signal and heard the resulting chaos, he hurried down a set of old stairs and opened the door to the basement. Seven exhausted, gaunt people, an older man, a middle-aged man and woman, and four children ranging in age from four to seventeen, stumbled out into the night air. The older man stumbled and the man with the scarf caught his elbow.

"Thank you," murmured the old man, in Yiddish, and then in French.

Each family member wore all the clothes they owned, and each had a book tucked into their skirts or shirts, whatever they wore. The seventeen-year-old secured the copy of The Golem inside his jacket.

The man with the coat and scarf urged them forward into a waiting truck and took off into the night.

Kathryn watched the burning books, smiling.

Andrew J. Lucas

Ocean's Bounty

Though nightmares vaulted, dreamscapes ply,
And with intent through ether fly.
The King in Yellow

IT WAS IN OCTOBER OF 1940 that our ship the *Ocean's Bounty* first answered the call. The captain, a career Naval officer recently foisted upon us by the Admiralty was thrilled to serve. The rest of us had been pulled away from our own ships, our families and our livelihood. To us, the shanghaied, the war was simply a pay cheque. We were late to the game and our small tramp was unable to meet the minimum speed required to join the Canadian escorted convoys, but that didn't stop us —no sir. Cpt. Whitaker insisted on taking to the North Atlantic without a military escort and a desperate War Department took us on. Of course, they only allowed us to move cargo of a lesser strategic importance, fully expecting we would probably never make port. We'd crossed the Atlantic three times by February of 1941 without even spotting a friendly ship, let alone a German. Each time the British had shaken their heads at our ramshackle wreck of a converted fishing boat and dutifully unloaded our shipment of tinned meat, condensed milk, and various sundry goods. I suppose the brass expected we would fall prey to a Kraut U-boat, and I guess in a way we did.

Outside, the night was clear and a full moon illuminated the dark swells of the North Atlantic. It was a perfect night for U-boats to hunt, but in spite of the danger, morale was high. We were doing our part for the war effort and the crew felt that a small ship like ours would be ignored by the Germans in favour of the plump pickings of the convoy ahead of us. The rest of the crew were below decks nursing our temperamental engines or enjoying each other's company in the ship's mess. The seas were high that night and Frankie Ramirez, our radio operator, was keeping me company on the bridge.

Frankie was a jumpy sort, obsessed with trying to keep in contact with whatever convoy the *Ocean's Bounty* was racing to keep up with. One passage during that summer, we had been leapfrogged by three entire convoys, one after the other. Frankie told us later when two of those were attacked by German submarines and many of the faster ships were sent to the bottom of the Atlantic. Jean Paul, the engineer, who was always cursing the reliability of our engines, espoused that our slow crawl and the solitude of our travel made us almost invisible to the submariners, whereas a loud cruiser-escorted convoy practically screamed for attention. Personally, I just hoped our luck held out until the war ended, but in 1941 that didn't seem likely to happen anytime soon, especially as our neighbours to the south were reluctant to join the fun.

This trip we were carrying pallets of tinned goods, salted meats, and a few barrels of fresh vegetables. We had all stocked up on the various contraband that would make us popular in port when we arrived. Halifax had a thriving underground industry providing Canadian whiskey, Hershey's chocolate, and packs of Lucky Strikes to industrious mariners. Frankie had gotten into my stock and was generously offering me a fag while he delicately searched the radio dial for a signal. I knew better than to complain or distract him from his task.

"Cheers, Frankie," I said as I graciously accepted one of my own cigarettes. "Anything?"

Frankie had one ear covered by the radio's headset and the other cupped by the hand which held his own dangling cigarette. I watched the glowing end of his cigarette as it slowly advanced up the bending tube of ash suspended between his fingers. It was a little aggravating watching him waste my cigarettes, when each one of them was worth a pint or a dance in an English pub.

"Maybe."

Frankie was a man of few words but he had a way with the radio which was uncanny. He could coax a signal out of thin air. Tonight he was listening to something and I'd found it was always best not to break his concentration. Whatever the radio was picking up must have been a music program or something, because Frankie was singing along with whatever he was hearing.

"Ph'nglui mglw'nafh," he whispered.

He must have been picking up a French free radio channel, because what he was singing certainly wasn't English.

"Cthulhu R'lyeh."

He sure as hell couldn't hold a tune. He was so bad that the hairs on the back of my neck were standing on end.

"Wgah'nagl fhtagn."

Frankie was butchering the song so much that I couldn't recognize the song and the words didn't seem like anything a human voice could produce let alone a language we could understand.

"Frankie!" I'd had enough.

"Eh?" he seemed distracted.

"Shut up! You're driving me crazy."

Frankie seemed confused, I guess he didn't realize he'd been singing along to whatever tune he'd been so engrossed in.

"Adjust course," Frankie suddenly snarled.

"Huh?"

"Adjust the fucking course!" he screamed as he abandoned his seat where he had been perched over the radio for the last few hours and scrambled to the wheel.

His sudden burst of activity took me by surprise, as did Frankie's strength as he heaved me aside. He spun the wheel hand-over-hand pulling the ship into a tight turn that threw me hard to the deck plates. Frankie braced himself against the bulkheads, squinting to see into the dark beyond the bridge's glass windows. I dragged myself to my feet just in time to see a mammoth shadow slide along the left side of the ship, eclipsing the moon and stars as it passed. A moment later the boat rocked violently to port, rising a good meter or so into the air before savagely crashing back into the water.

This time I managed to retain my footing. I was scared beyond measure and shaking from adrenaline.

"What the hell was that, Frankie?"

"*Cthulhu R'lyeh,*" Frankie whispered under his breath.

"Frankie? Snap out of it!" I shouted, shaking him. After a moment his eyes focused on me again.

"What the hell was that?" I shouted at him again.

"I don't know."

In apparent answer, a grinding noise followed by a deep thud came from somewhere below deck. We looked at each other in terror, knowing full well that a torpedo hit was a death sentence for any ship alone on the Atlantic. Frankie frantically shut down the engines while I grabbed the bridge's set of binoculars and rushed out to foredeck, intent on finding out what was out there. I probably should have headed in the opposite direction down into the engine room, but I had to know what that shadow was.

It wasn't hard to find as right off the port bow of the Ocean's Bounty was my worst fear—a German U-boat. The German's conning tower was almost level with our bridge and I could imagine a Kraut submariner lining up a salvo. That sheer wall of metal heaved and shuddered in the ocean swell and I could see a broad swath of shiny metal where our keel had scraped across the spine of the submarine. The damage didn't look that severe, but here and there I could spot equipment mounts and railings which had been bent or ripped off the fin by our strike. The U-boat looked sound but I could only imagine what the effect of this close a strike had been on our own ship.

As if in answer to this thought, a second resounding boom echoed through the ship, and a blast of heat and smoke billowed up from below decks. I headed off at a run realizing that there was nothing I could do about the Germans. They would sink the ship or not, but unless I got below right away the *Ocean's Bounty* was either going to sink or explode on its own.

I wasn't wrong. The ship was taking on water and the engines were aflame by the time I got below. Frankie had joined Jean Paul and together they were operating the ancient hand-pumped fire equipment. They seemed to have the blaze under control and a third pair of hands would have only gotten in the way, so I sought out the captain and the rest of the crew. The mess had taken the brunt of the damage and the collision had pushed a beam directly against the hatch and sealed the crew within. It was horrific. They had all been enjoying their supper in the mess. I could see my captain and the whole rest of my crewmates through the porthole, suspended in the frigid seawater that had poured in. As I sealed the mess compartment, securely entombing my captain and crewmates, I reminded myself that I still had two men fighting to keep the engines from exploding and a German sub on the verge of blowing us up.

A frantic hour or so later the three of us were standing on the foredeck considering our options and staring at the impassive expanse of dull grey metal that had killed 13 of our comrades and crippled our ship. It hadn't taken the opportunity to put a torpedo into our side or unlimber its deck gun, but it also hadn't taken any initiative to help us either. The U-boat sat a few meters off our bow, as stoic and unmoving as a rocky

Newfoundland shoal. I took note of the ship's designation, U-587, hoping I wouldn't take those numbers to my grave.

"Jean Paul."

"Aye, sir."

I could tell the man was fatigued. Fighting the fire, breathing in god knows what, and watching his comrades drown had obviously taken a toll on the usually vivacious Acadian.

"How are the engines?"

Jean Paul considered the question a moment before responding.

"They'll get us to Liverpool if we're lucky."

"Okay," I responded, hoping to project a confidence I really didn't feel. "Frankie, get me that Chicago Typewriter you keep behind your bunk."

"Sir?"

Frankie had bartered a few cases of good Canadian Whiskey for a Thompson submachine gun on our last trip. Every now and then the crew would take turns burning rounds into the ocean swells on clear days. It could send a whole clip of ammo within a minute down range up to 50 meters. Where I was going, I didn't expect to need anywhere near that range.

"Look. That U-boat hasn't moved for almost two hours." I explained. "Either it was crippled when we hit it, or it's waiting for us to move away before plunking one in our side while we're unawares. Either way if it gets underway before we do we're dead."

"But..." Jean Paul began.

"No buts. Someone has to check it out. You have to nurse those engines back to working order. Frankie you try to get someone on the radio."

"I'll try, but all I'm getting is some foreign program."

Frankie looked rattled, and I couldn't blame him but we were desperate. If there was a British ship anywhere nearby, I needed Frankie to get them on the horn. I put a hand on his shoulder and pulled him close. The contact seemed to steady him.

"Look, you did good seeing that German bastard at all..."

"I didn't see it, the radio warned me," Frankie protested.

"If we'd hit it dead on we wouldn't even be talking about it right now."

Jean Paul and I set about preparing the mooring lines and Frankie went to retrieve his submachine gun, still muttering about the radio. Poor guy. He was obviously shaken by the night's events, I just hoped he could hold it together while I boarded the U-boat. I didn't want to have to worry about him losing it when I was about to board an enemy vessel.

Once the *Ocean's Bounty* had been secured along-side the U-boat, I had no choice but to board it. I didn't know much about U-boats but I expected they had more than enough crew to repel a single Canadian merchant marine. My only real hope was to negotiate with the German submariners. The Thompson was meant to make my argument just that bit more persuasive.

I girded my loins, as it were, threw open the upper lock, and trained my weapon down into the conning tower.

I wasn't immediately greeted by gun fire, which I took as a good sign. I threw a cautious thumbs up to Frankie, who was watching anxiously from the *Ocean's Bounty's* bridge, and went in. I tried to keep the Thompson pointed down as I climbed the ladder rungs, but was forced to sling or I'd slip and break my neck. My rational mind told me that the Germans hadn't emerged to exercise their superior firepower for a reason. Perhaps they wanted to negotiate, perhaps they didn't want to attack us, and perhaps, just perhaps, the boat was adrift and deserted. It was unlikely that I was venturing down this dark steel hole simply to be met with a volley of lead, but I was still heading into a dark steel hole and my gut knew it.

I descended quickly, sliding down the iron ladder and coming up hard against the steel hatch sealing the U-boat. I took a deep breath to steady myself, then cranked the handwheel to open it. The hatch made a god-awful screech as I lifted it, that surely alerted every German seaman within that I was about to enter. The air inside assaulted me with stench of such foulness that it brought me to my knees. It was only with the utmost of self-control that I stopped myself from heaving my breakfast upon the Nazi deck. I'd heard from a British submariner I'd once met in Plymouth that submarines were renowned for their ability to capture and magnify all the assorted odors associated with running a sealed canister filled with heavy equipment, fuel, chemicals, and sweating humanity— but this was beyond the pale.

Preparing myself as best I could, I wrapped my thick, woollen scarf about my mouth and nose, which was of scant help blocking that all-pervasive putrid stench, but the smell of the wool distracted such that I could enter that charnel house. And a charnel house it was, the conning tower was occupied with the corpses of three German seamen, each evidently had died of exposure or dehydration. They were huddled against the outer lock like they had been attempting to escape the constraints of their vessel—unsuccessfully it seemed.

The conning tower was joined to the main hull by a second water-tight hatch that someone, perhaps these three dead men, had jammed by inserting a pry bar into the opening mechanism. With the bar jammed into the wheel, it was securely sealed, though it was simple enough to unjam by removing the iron bar. I wondered why the three men hadn't done so. Perhaps in their half-starved and weakened state their minds simply didn't register that they could unjam the hatch and escape, or they were too weak to do so. I hefted the heavy tool for a moment and discounted that theory, for as heavy as the iron was, a child would have been able to push it out of the position it had been wedged into.

I could not fathom what would have driven men to such an act of insanity or what would have kept their crewmates from rushing to their aid.

It took me only a moment to dislodge the pry bar and enter the U-boat. In comparison to the conning tower, the boat's control centre was a breath of air. Stale, and laden with the smells of a working vessel to be sure, but without the cloying reek of death and madness. The room was illuminated by a few dim gauges and a single bulb above one of the instrument panels. The boat rocked gently in the grip of the ocean's swells. I moved about the control room looking for signs of life, or at least occupation, but there were none, aside from that single light bulb.

The rest of the equipment within the control room was inactive, except for this one station. Now I was no military type, but like all seamen I recognized a radio when I saw one. This one was very similar to the equipment on the *Ocean's Bounty,* having all the requisite dials, switches, and levers. Except for the

Germanic labels on the dials it could have been taken from a British or Canadian ship. The major difference was a strange rotary typewriter and a reel-to-reel tape recorder next to the radio and plugged into the receiver. The tape deck's use was obvious, and I supposed that this close to England the vessel had been spying on Commonwealth radio traffic. As to the use of the typewriter, I was baffled as it seemed incomplete: there was no paper feed, and where a carriage return should have been was a bizarre arrangement of moving rotors. I tapped a few keys, saw how they produced lights under other keys, but never the same light when I pressed the same key multiple times.

It was beyond strange and had a hunch that this would be something that the Admiralty would be interested in seeing. I closed the typewriter into the sturdy case that housed it and sealed it shut. I was picking up the case and a stack of official looking documents and journals scattered about the station when I heard a sound behind me. Turning, I saw a dishevelled German dressed in heavily stained coveralls. Both of us looked surprised to see the other. We stood silently for a moment, wondering if the other was real or a trick of the imagination. It was the German who broke the silence.

"*Schwein! Lassen Sie mich!*" he shouted, spittle spraying from his mouth as he moved towards me, eyes wild.

I looked about for my weapon and spied it directly behind the man, lying upon an arrangement of nautical maps and navigation equipment. It might as well have been back on the *Ocean's Bounty* for all the good it did me. The German ignored the gun and moved towards me with cold intent in his eyes and balled fists raised.

The man was brown with caked dirt and oil, and his coveralls had huge brown stains down the front whose origin I could only guess at. I stepped back, hesitant to engage him.

"Cthulhu wgah'nagl fhtagn," he growled as he lunged at me.

The words, while strangely familiar, were gibberish, but his eyes showed the madness within. On pure instinct I swung the heavy case I was carrying, striking the charging Kraut directly in the temple. He fell heavily, a dark purple bruise maring his terror-filled face. He fell to the deck and struggled to regain his footing, one hand clasping his damaged face. I was shocked at the damage I had inflicted, but the type-writer was sturdily built and my fear-fuelled blow should have stunned the man. Yet he was trying to regain feet and was even now on his knees. In a moment he would be coming at me again. I swung the German typewriter again, striking him in the same location, deepening the cavity I had created with my first hit. Blood and gore erupted from the wound and the man fell again.

I struck again and again until his skull collapsed inward and grey matter and crimson blood coated the typewriter case. I stood above him, trying to regain my calm, not that being enclosed in an enemy vessel had allowed me any real sense of calm to begin with, and grabbed Freddie's Tommy, vowing to keep it close at hand from then on. The weapon was cold and heavy, but allowed my confidence to return in spite of the gore-covered body at my feet.

"Cthulhu verzeihen. Ihre vassel winkt." The German wheezed at my feet and shuddered.

Jumping back, I reflexively pulled the trigger on

the machine gun but nothing happened—I had left the safety on during my climb into the U-boat and forgotten to take it off—stupid. At my feet the German chanted something through his ruined face, a supplication to our Lord perhaps. Fearfully, I struggled to release the safety on the unfamiliar weapon, stepping back as I did so. I dropped the typewriter so I could use both hands to fiddle with the latch and just as I had the weapon primed, the German was on his feet, staring at me through what remained of his face, shouting again with a spray of bloody froth.

"Ihre vassel winkt!"

He lunged at me and I pulled frantically on the trigger of the Thompson. A dozen rounds or so peppered the man, ripping flesh away from his body from his chest to his face. Blood, gore, and viscera exploded from the man, coating the walls and instruments behind him. He fell again and I held the trigger down until the magazine emptied. There was little recognizable of him than a lump of mishappen gore when I was done. Panting, I shouldered the weapon and stepped back from my ghastly handiwork.

I had no idea if the man had been alone or not, but any element of stealth I may have had was now gone. I had surely alerted the entire crew with my fireworks and it was imperative that I get out of the vessel now while I still had the chance. I picked up the typewriter, journals, and a handful of maps and turned towards the conning tower, my mind on escape. Holding my captured booty close to my chest with one hand, I slung the Thompson over my shoulder with the other and gripped the iron ladder, making to pull myself up and out to safety.

"Verzeihen R'Lyeh," came a moist whisper from

behind me.

I looked back. The mutilated corpse was shuddering and convulsing. I stared in horrific disbelief as the corpse staggered to its feet. Its shredded muscles barely supported it, and here and there bright bone was plainly exposed, yet it stood. More than that, it began shuffling towards me, despite the intestines and gore pouring from its abdomen. I scrambled up the ladder and slammed the hatch shut, turning the wheel hard to secure it. A moment later, an object of unearthly strength threw itself against the hatch, causing it to shudder against my back. I scrambled to pick up the pry bar and only just got it in place just before the creature on the other side started to twist the locking wheel in the opposite direction. Desperate, I jammed the pry bar into the wheel, praying it would jam the mechanism. The wheel caught the metal bar. It bent slightly, but it held.

Safe for the moment, I rested my head against the cold metal, attempting to rally my mind against the horror I had just escaped. I struggled to draw breath into my lungs, to calm my racing heart. I rubbed my eyes with my fists, willing my body and mind to calm, to make sense of what I had just escaped. Nothing in our training or my life had prepared me to face a creature that could absorb that much punishment and still keep coming.

It was with these thoughts dominating my mind that I left the U-boat behind, sealing the conning tower's hatch one last time. Frankie and Jean Paul were waiting for me aboard the *Ocean's Bounty*. Jean Paul lifted me back to the ship, supporting my fear-weakened body with a firm hand. In the crisp North Atlantic air the horrors I had encountered below quickly receded from my tortured mind. Surely it had been only a trick of the light and my own fearful mind that had interpreted my fight with the Kraut in such a ghastly way. I was no soldier; perhaps my response was typical of a man seeing combat for the first time.

I ordered our ship to make for England at our best possible speed, barely a crawl, but I wanted, no, *needed,* to be away from that vessel and what it contained. We lacked the ability to scuttle the German U-boat, and it there was still a good chance that our own ship would take on more water and sink. Our only hope was to travel as far and as fast as we could manage and hope that we would be able to intercept a friendly convoy before our engines gave out. We'd try for England's shores, but none of us really expected to make it.

As the *Ocean's Bounty* made way, I watched the bobbing tower of the U-boat recede beyond the horizon, and with it the horrors it contained. I hoped it would be sunk upon sighting by the Royal Navy, sending it and its inhuman crew to the depths where they belonged.

Frankie and I manned the bridge while Jean Paul struggled below decks, nursing the engines. I looked forward, searching for sight of land, while Frankie, now inseparable from his Tommy gun, searched the airwaves for a friendly signal. The dull throb of the labouring engines was soothing, but Frankie's incessant crooning got on my nerves.

"*Ph'nglui mglw'nafh,*" Frankie whispered to himself, as he tuned the radio to an emergency frequency. He ceased his song long enough to send out a distress call. "Mayday, any ships within range, please respond."

He listened for a response for a minute or so, whispering his foreign song all the while, then he moved to another channel. I noticed he kept his finger on the transmitter button while scanning the radio bands. I suppose this was to keep the channel active in case someone was out there listening on some arcane, obscure frequency. If they didn't hear his mayday they would no doubt hear his humming.

"Frankie, anything on the radio?"

Frankie turned to me from where he was hunched over his radio. The morning sun outlined his gaunt face, no doubt as wide-eyed and haunted a visage as my own. It was dawn. Had it only been a single night?

"Nothing, Sir." he whispered, intent upon his equipment.

"Well, keep at it."

Frankie fiddled with the radio, drawing a warbling crackle from it as he delicately moved its dials. He was engrossed in his work and our lives might well depend upon his coaxing a response from the machine. I left him alone and looked out over the ocean. It was breathtaking in the dawn light, the unbroken horizon holding promises and hope. It seemed only a matter of time before a silhouette of a friendly ship crested in the distance. Beneath me the deck shuddered in time with the labouring engines but I knew the ship would hold together long enough to make port or until Frankie's radio picked up a friendly transmission. The radio howled as the frequency shifted, produced a staccato, almost rhythmic clicking, before settling into static. If anyone could coax something from that cacophony it would be Frankie. Hopefully something other than that incessant tune he was still humming.

Though I had to admit, it was starting to grow on me.

Dawn Vogel

NOCHNAYA
SERENADA

THE THING ROZALIYA HATED most about being
Erina's navigator was she could never see the ground
beneath them, as Erina flew their wood and canvas
biplane perfectly parallel to the ground. It made her job
nearly impossible and left her feeling superfluous.

On top of that, Erina didn't appreciate Rozaliya's
humming to pass the time.

"Would you cease that infernal claptrap?" Erina
sputtered over the wind whistling through the biplane's
wings.

"It isn't claptrap. I am serenading you with a
wonderful waltz. I thought it apropos, as we are to
bomb the composer's countrymen."

Erina's tone grew sharp. "If your wonderful
composer was alive today, would he be saluting us or
Der Führer?" Erina made the German words sound

wretched, like curses upon the earth and all who dwelt there.

Rozaliya frowned. She didn't want to argue with Erina. Erina was one of the best pilots in the 46th, and she'd never failed to return them home without a scratch on them or their plane. Hoping to divert her pilot's attention, she asked, "We should nearly be to our target, should we not?"

A sharp tapping came from the cockpit, followed by Erina clearing her throat. "Er, the clock has stopped. I thought we fixed it."

"Nothing in this hunk of junk stays fixed for long." A glint of light off the starboard wings drew her attention. "Did Olga send more than just us?"

"She said only one plane for this mission."

Rozaliya watched for what could only be another plane, but the cloud cover was increasing. "Fly faster," she murmured, too softly for Erina to hear.

Normally, her magic had no effect on machinery. Nonetheless, she felt a tingle in her fingertips, and their plane sped up.

The burst of speed would have been to their advantage if she hadn't noticed the other plane too late. It emerged from a cloudbank and released a hail of bullets into the side of their rickety plane. No bullets hit Rozaliya, and that Erina did not cry out suggested either the pilot had also not been hit, or the bullets aimed toward her had killed her instantly.

Regardless, the plane was going down.

* * *

Rozaliya crawled from the wreckage as soon as the plane had finished digging a long, wide furrow through the German countryside. Her arms and legs collapsed beneath her, and she crumpled to the ground, the earthy loam filling her senses. Beneath her fingers, the soil felt as it did in the Motherland, but they had crossed the border some time before. The earth still comforted her, and she let herself slip toward unconsciousness.

Erina.

Rozaliya jolted from her torpor and looked around. The landscape swam before her eyes, blurring the brown of the earth with the brown of their plane, with the brown of Erina's hair, jacket, and cap. Rozaliya reached toward what she thought was Erina, but her fingers touched nothing.

She awoke to men's voices, speaking German. She lay still on the ground, now cold beneath her body, and peered out from behind slit eyelids.

"This one's still breathing," one of the voices reported from somewhere in the distance. They must be talking about Erina, not her.

"Good, we'll take her in." The second voice had a hard edge to it. "What about the other?"

Rozaliya gulped in a breath, remained curled up and unmoving, her face turned toward the earth. Let the dirt fill her nostrils, if she must. Anything to convince them she no longer lived.

Something jabbed at her side, but she lay as though she were little more than a log on the ground.

"This one's not moving," a third voice said. Young, not skilled enough yet to notice that she breathed through her nose and tried not to shiver.

"Then there is no sense in dragging her corpse back to camp. Let it rot here with this contraption the Russians seem to think is a plane."

Rozaliya allowed her eyelids to open just a fraction

more, so she could see these men and which direction they were taking Erina. She wanted to shoot them, but Erina always made her leave her pistol in her bunk.

One of the German soldiers tossed Erina over his shoulder like a sack of potatoes. There was a kübelwagen nearby, still running, that Rozaliya had slept through arriving. The officer, wearing a heavier coat and looking better groomed than the two soldiers, took Erina, placed her in the front seat of the kübelwagen, and smoothed a curl away from her face.

"A pretty one, eh?" He was the sharp-voiced man, and his laughter matched. The others joined in, but it was the officer's laughter that chilled Rozaliya's bones.

He turned toward Rozaliya, and she feared she must have whimpered against her will. He shook his head. "We'll have to come back and burn this thing once we've gotten her back to camp."

Rozaliya committed his face to memory. She'd be long gone before he returned, but that didn't mean she wouldn't find him again.

* * *

The kübelwagen had moved too quickly for Rozaliya to follow on foot, but there was only one road nearby, and she had seen which way the kübelwagen had gone. She followed the road in that direction until she heard a vehicle in the distance, which drove her back to the rough earth alongside the road. As the kübelwagen drew nearer, she recognized the same men who had taken Erina, though Rozaliya's pilot was no longer in the vehicle.

Again, she wished for her pistol. Magic had nothing on cold steel. A few quick shots into the tires to disable their vehicle, and then she could murder these

Nazis, one by one.

Instead, she turned up the collar of her worn wool jacket, covering the lower portion of her face. She rose and waved, and the kübelwagen slowed to a stop beside her.

Muttering an incantation under her breath to make the men believe she looked appropriate to her surroundings, and also to amplify her natural charm, she looked at the driver. "Give a girl a ride?" The less German she spoke, the better—though she knew their language, her accent might give her away as Russian.

The driver began to nod, but the officer sitting beside him shook his head and placed a hand on the driver's shoulder.

"No, no rides."

Rozaliya focused on the officer, the same one who had moved the curl from Erina's face. At his throat, he wore a medallion bearing a stylized pillar and a series of runes. She didn't recognize their origin, other than Nordic, but it didn't seem to matter. Her magic wasn't working on him. She nodded. "Sorry to trouble you."

As Rozaliya walked back into the field, the kübelwagen continued toward the wreckage of the plane. Rozaliya hazarded a glance in their direction, and was unsurprised to see the officer still staring at her. She hoped he hadn't studied her face as well as she'd studied his.

By the time she came upon the downed plane, it was a bonfire, and the kübelwagen was again driving away, heading farther down the road toward where she now noticed a steeple. A town.

She followed, kept upright now by her anger. She hummed under her breath as she went, now that Erina wasn't here to complain about her humming. She had been fed a steady diet of opera as a child, thanks to her grandmother's roots in that art form. Now, the songs of revenge sung by women and men alike filled her brain and drove her forward.

* * *

The town was full of Nazi kübelwagens, but she found the one she was looking for parked outside a ramshackle building. As the door thumped open, the smell of schnapps, the tune of a piano, and the flash of glittery clothing all wafted out.

A cabaret.

Rozaliya's eyes widened. She'd heard about the German cabarets, but never dreamed she might see one. And the Nazis who had taken Erina were likely inside.

She slipped around to the back of the building just as a gaggle of chorus girls, their faces made up with exaggerated lips and eyes, poured out the back door, lighting cigarettes and shivering in the cold.

Rozaliya moved toward the door, gaze on the ground, the collar of her wool jacket turned up again.

"You're late," one of the chorus girls said, a sneer pasted across her features.

"Sorry," Rozaliya said.

The woman pulled the door open wider. "You'd better get ready fast. We've got five minutes until we're on next."

Rozaliya nodded and ducked beneath the woman's arm. The backstage area was dim, and she stumbled over random detritus as she searched for the dressing room.

A full rack of chorus girl costumes greeted her within, and she stripped and redressed in a flimsy glittery blouse and short skirt that matched what the other girls were wearing, tucking her flying clothing into a corner beneath a broken feather fan. A quick glance in the mirror assured her she looked frightful, but there wasn't time to do much more than run her fingers through her short hair before she pulled on a headband, pinch her cheeks, and bite her lips.

And then the dressing room was filled with other young women, chattering and giggling in rapid-fire German. Rozaliya followed well enough to catch the instructions about lining up, choreography, and the song they'd be singing, an old bierhaus standard.

She didn't know the words, but she smiled, moved her mouth, and kicked at the appropriate times. And watched the crowd for her targets.

The stage lighting was bright enough, and the cabaret dark enough, that the men in the audience were but silhouettes facing the dancing girls. But the song went by in a blur as Rozaliya stared out into the crowd, a smile plastered across her face, searching for her quarry.

As the song reached the final chorus, the girls on either end of the stage began descending into the crowd, stopping at some of the tables near the stage to favor the gentlemen with smiles and delicate hands placed on shoulders. Rozaliya's smile became genuine as she followed their lead.

Picking her way through the crowded maze of tables, she paused long enough to share a flirtatious smile with the men, long enough to get a good look at their faces and determine they were not the one she was looking for.

Finally, she spotted him. The officer who had moved Erina's curl from her face, calling her pretty and sneering at the same time. A quick glance at the other cabaret girls confirmed what Rozaliya had hoped. A number of them were now seated with the men in the club, some on tables, some on laps, some on abandoned chairs, while other girls were dancing with the men to the faint strains of the band, overlain by chattering, laughter, and beer steins clinking. Here in the heart of the Axis powers, there was merriment aplenty.

Not for Rozaliya.

She moved toward the Nazi officer, singing as she walked.

"Not only are you the God of mercy,
And forgiving grace, but also in your anger
God of battle and of vengeance,
For as that God I worship you,
Oh hearken, hear my prayer!
I had no soul in the world except my sister,
No parents, no husband, no, none that could replace her,
She has been stolen from me, she has been ruin'd,
Oh let me find the man and have my revenge on him;
Lord, who is not only the God of mercy,
And of pardon, oh hearken, hear my prayer!"

"What is that song?" a man asked as he grabbed her arm and spun her around. He stank of beer and stale sweat as he leaned in close to her face. "What is that beautiful song?"

"It's from *Doktor Faust.*" Rozaliya favored him with an artificial smile. "Do you like it?"

"I like your voice. Will you sing for us more?" He gestured to a table filled with other young men, all looking as inebriated as he was.

Rozaliya shook her head. "I'm sorry, I've got to get to the bar now."

"Just one more song?" he pleaded.

"Sorry, I can't." She tried to pull away from him, but his grip on her arm grew tighter.

"Then what good are you?" he asked, spittle flying from his lips.

That spurred Rozaliya into action. She shoved him away with her free hand and stomped her heel onto the toe of his boot at the same moment.

In his shock, he let go of her arm, but then reached out for her again.

Rozaliya scooted backward, just in time to move past a dancing couple, who interposed themselves between the drunk man and her. When he grabbed again, his hand fell on the officer's sleeve, bringing the dance to a halt. Rozaliya didn't stick around to see the aftermath, but continued on toward the officer she had identified.

The false smile plastered onto her face again, she batted her eyelashes as she reached his table. "Hey there, soldier," she said, draping an arm across his shoulder.

Though his body tensed beneath her arm, he favored her with a smile. "What is your name, darling?"

"You may call me darling if you like."

"Very well." His lips twitched toward a frown. "Your accent, where are you from?"

"Debrecen," she said, gaze downward. The city was far enough from where they were now and recently destroyed, so she hoped he would not pursue it further.

"Ah, my condolences."

"I would rather not think of it tonight." Steeling herself, she asked, "Might I interest you in a walk instead?"

He inclined his head toward the stage. "Don't you have more dancing to do?"

"Not soon enough to interrupt a short walk." She glanced around, feigning nervousness. "The bosses don't want us girls to smoke in the club. We have to go outside."

He smiled and rose from his chair, presenting an arm to her. "Then we shall take the air. But, I insist, when we are outside, you must tell me your name."

Rozaliya smiled and took his arm. "Rosa," she whispered, as they slipped out into the street.

"Pretty name for a pretty girl."

She pulled closer to him as a gust of wind, chilly in the early spring, raised her skin into goose pimples. "Can I get one of your cigarettes?"

He pulled a pack from his pocket, allowed her to take one, and tucked another between his narrow lips before lighting it. Then he leaned close to her and lit her cigarette off his, his cold blue eyes boring into her dark eyes.

Rozaliya glanced away. It was easy to look embarrassed under his penetrating gaze. She didn't want him to look too deeply into her soul, lest he see the truth of her plan. "Where shall we walk?" Her voice was husky from the first drag off her cigarette. The German tobacco was fragrant, so much better than the stale cigarettes she and the other girls had smuggled into their camp.

"That depends on what you have in mind, Rosa," he said, winking at her.

Rozaliya arched her eyebrow. "I thought you were concerned about me getting back to dance, earlier. And anyway, I still don't know your name."

"Friedrich. Are you allowed schnapps in the cabaret?"

Rozaliya froze, unsure of the answer, but she recovered and shook her head. It might not be true, but he wouldn't have asked if he already knew. "No, no drinking on the job. Though I'd rather have vodka."

"Vodka?" He grimaced. "Vodka is forbidden. At least until Russia is defeated."

The words 'Mother Russia will never be defeated' leapt to her tongue unbidden, but she kept them from escaping her lips by swallowing hard, as though the words themselves were a strong drink. They burned going down, just the same. "Of course. Schnapps is just so sweet."

"You don't like it?"

"No, but if you give me schnapps, I'll drink it."

"Then come with me to my room, and I'll share my schnapps with you."

She blushed, and the reaction was real. Officer or not, she should not accept his invitation to join him in his room. Her family would be scandalized, and the priests would never forgive such an act.

Then again, she planned to murder him, as soon as she knew where to find Erina. So perhaps the state of her immortal soul was of less concern. She gave him a shy nod and allowed him to take her by the hand.

* * *

The room was small, but it was still far more space than Rozaliya was accustomed to in the women's barracks. Friedrich kissed her as soon they were inside the room, and she took her time prying herself away from him, certain she could wrap him around her finger even without magic.

"Lie on the bed." Rozaliya gently pushed him away as she reached for the buttons on the front of her borrowed costume.

"Don't you want some schnapps first?"

"Later."

Once he was on the bed, she undid her buttons slowly, not removing the shirt, but letting it hang from her shoulders, just covering her bare breasts.

A flush crept over his pale skin as she bent over, rolling down her stockings and removing them. Stretching them out in front of her, she smiled and sauntered toward the bed.

She unbuttoned his uniform shirt, peeling it off his arms, and punctuating the motion with delicate kisses. She tried not to look at the pendant he wore, the thing that prevented her from using her magical charms on him. Her mundane charms would suffice tonight.

When his shirt was off, she lifted his wrist to the wooden bedframe and wrapped her stocking around both.

"What are you doing?" he asked, resisting her grip.

"Relax, darling. You'll enjoy it more this way." Rozaliya finished knotting one stocking. She straddled his chest and began tying up his other wrist as she kissed him. When she was finished, his breath came in shuddering pants.

"See?"

"Oh yes."

"Good." She climbed off Friedrich and the bed, unbuckling his belt as she did. She pulled it from his belt loops and moved to the foot of the bed, where she slung his belt around her neck and began to unlace his boots. But rather than pulling them from his feet, she tied the partially unlaced boots snug to his feet, and then to the bedframe.

With Friedrich restrained, she pulled his pistol from the holster he had set down with his jacket and tucked it into the waistband of her short skirt.

He gulped, choking down air. "What are you doing?" he gasped.

"Don't worry, darling. Tell me what I want to know, and I promise I'll make it quick." She leapt from where she stood to the bed and sat hard on his upper chest. Seized with a sudden aching to bend his will to her own, her fingers fumbled at the chain that held the talisman close to his throat, but they found no clasp anywhere along its length.

"You will not take my faith in the Old Ways from me, even if you kill me."

Rozaliya laughed. "Old Ways? My ways are the Old Ways. Yours are misguided. But don't take my laughter at your belief to mean I won't kill you. You'd best start talking. What did you do with the downed pilot?"

"Who?"

Rozaliya sighed. "Don't play dumb, Friedrich."

He shrugged in spite of his restraints. "But I don't know what you're talking about."

Threading his belt behind his neck, she began to cinch it around his throat, blocking her view of his talisman. Her inability to see it didn't negate its power, but at least she didn't have to look at the damn thing, stupid Aryan magic that somehow counteracted her spells. "Let's try this again. You found a pilot in a downed Russian aircraft earlier, yes?"

He started to nod, which tightened the belt at his throat. "Yes," he gasped.

Rozaliya loosened the belt's tension, just enough so Friedrich wasn't prevented from breathing. "Where did you take her?"

"Who are you?"

She looked at him and shook her head, tightening the belt a touch. "Try again. Where did you take her?"

Friedrich's gaze narrowed. "You are Russian?"

"Oh yes. But you're not answering my question." She pulled the pistol from her waistband, leaned back, and tapped the barrel against his left kneecap. "Do you like walking? Then tell me where you took her."

"We just took her back to camp. She'll be held there until they try her as an enemy combatant."

She watched him, loosening the belt slightly more. He sweated profusely, his face pale, and his eyes wide with fear. She had no reason to doubt the information he was giving her. "Very good. Do you prefer strangulation or a gunshot?" She paused, quirking one side of her mouth into a smile. "I am a navigator, not a markswoman. It might take a few gunshots."

"No, don't kill me, please. I will take you to her."

"Sorry, Friedrich. I'm sure you would take me right there, but that won't get her or me free of this wretched country and this wretched war. But you're sweet. I'll strangle you. The pain won't last long. And I'll sing to you, if you like."

"No, no, just let me go, you crazy woman!"

Rozaliya shook her head. "Stop being rude." She tightened the belt to cut off Friedrich's windpipe, preventing him from shouting.

"*Ah, flee the traitor, and let him cozen you no more,*" she sang, pulling the belt tighter still. Friedrich's tongue lolled from his mouth and his eyes began to bulge.

Rozaliya squeezed her eyes shut as she pulled, slowly rising to make the belt even tighter. "*Deceit is on his lips and falsehood in his eyes. From my suffering learn what it means to trust him—*"

His feeble attempts to free himself from the restraints or the strangulation abated.

She dropped the end of the belt, and spared Friedrich's body one last glance, his face purple and still. *"And be warned in time by my plight."*

* * *

By the time Rozaliya returned to the cabaret for her clothing, the officers and the girls were long gone. She'd ransacked Friedrich's things, hoping maybe he was holding out on the forbidden vodka, but she had only found the promised schnapps. Instead of drinking it, she'd poured it over his corpse and left a smoldering cigarette tucked between his lips. If she was lucky, all evidence of her having been there would be obliterated before anyone had a chance to look for her.

She hoped Friedrich's kübelwagen would still be parked outside, but there were no vehicles in sight when she came out the back door of the cabaret. Instead, she set out on foot in the direction the kübelwagen had come from.

She was glad for the heat of her anger as she made her way across the cold and barren landscape.

* * *

The borders of the Nazi camp were not well guarded. Rozaliya watched for a long time, just to make sure her assessment was correct, but no guards patrolled the outer edges of their tents.

Rozaliya slipped into a tent, found a discarded uniform, and changed her clothing, bundling her own clothes into a knapsack this time. Once her hair was tucked beneath a soldier's cap, she checked her reflection in a polished piece of tin. So long as she kept her head down and didn't speak, she'd do well enough to blend in.

She had hoped for a pistol in the tent where she had found the uniform, but she hadn't lingered long enough to root through all the soldier's belongings, and she'd left behind Friedrich's pistol in his room. Since no weapon had presented itself, she went unarmed.

Her evaluation of the camp from outside had given her no sense of where they might be keeping prisoners within. There were no stockades, not even any permanent buildings in the area, save for a lone ramshackle barn, still stark white and red against the brown and gray landscape.

As she drew nearer, her heart surged with the surety that this was where the Nazis were keeping Erina. Two soldiers guarded the entrance, both carrying rifles. Rozaliya took a deep breath, muttering an incantation to help her to blend into her surroundings, as she approached the door.

"What's that?" one of the soldiers asked, jerking his head toward her knapsack.

"Medical supplies." She kept her voice quiet so as to not give away its higher pitch.

"For who?"

"Inside."

The two soldiers exchanged a glance, but one of them stepped toward the door and opened it for her.

"Thank you kindly." The moment the words had slipped past her lips, she was sure her overly polite German would draw unwanted attention. Neither soldier stopped her, though, so she continued into the barn.

The smell inside assured her she'd picked the wrong place, and the soldiers believed she was there to minister to a cow or horse within. As her eyes adjusted, though, Rozaliya saw the pale flesh of people, crowded into the stalls previously inhabited by the animals. The stench was a mixture of the uncleaned stalls and the human waste that now mingled with the animal waste.

She scanned the faces for Erina. None of them were right, all too thin, too hungry, too scared.

And then she saw her. Erina had shoved her way to the front of a stall and was staring at Rozaliya with unbridled hatred.

Rozaliya let out a half sob, half laugh, pulling her soldier's cap from her head. "It's me," she said in Russian.

The corner of Erina's mouth quirked up in a half smile. "Do you have a plan, little sister?"

Rozaliya blushed at her pilot's use of the nickname she'd earned around their camp, always helping out with the tasks of the other airwomen. Rozaliya nodded toward the back of the barn, to another set of doors. "Are those guarded as well?"

Erina shrugged. "One way to find out."

Rozaliya undid the latches that kept the wooden gate of the stall closed, releasing Erina and the prisoners who had been contained with her.

"You'll have to remain as quiet as you can," Rozaliya told Erina's stall-mates. "We can't let the guards know what we're planning."

The prisoners nodded, but as the two Russian women opened more stall gates, the prisoners reunited with friends and family members, and the volume of the crowd grew.

"Check the door," Erina said.

Rozaliya looked around for anything she might use as a weapon but saw nothing. But if nothing was done, the guards would come in soon, and though their rifles would not kill many prisoners, she suspected they would aim bullets at she and Erina as the obvious ringleaders.

She eased the door she had come through open just a crack and smiled at the soldier there. "Sleep, sweet prince," she said in Russian, wiggling her fingers in his direction.

Instead of slumping to the side, he peered at her more closely. "What was that?"

Rozaliya scrambled for the right words in German. Her magic normally worked regardless of any language barriers present, but tonight had not been a good night for her magic. She tried again in Russian, though she put more force behind her voice.

The soldier blinked several times before falling over.

"What?" The other soldier outside the building yanked open the door Rozaliya was hiding behind, gun pointed at her chest.

She lurched toward the now sleeping soldier and scrambled for his gun. Her sudden motion surprise the soldier who was still standing, and she was on her back, the sleeping soldier's pistol aimed at the other before he had even brought his gun around to bear on her new position.

"You can sleep too." She pulled the trigger.

Erina was at the door before Rozaliya was back on her feet. "What are you doing out here shooting the guards?"

"Making sure no one notices the noise inside."

"As though the other soldiers will not have heard that shot?"

Rozaliya sighed. "It was me or him, Erina."

Erina shook her head and helped Rozaliya to her

feet, leading her to the larger central area of the barn. There, Erina addressed the assembled prisoners in German. "Anyone who can fight will follow Roza and me out the back doors. If we encounter any soldiers, the rest of you should keep moving. There's a copse of woods not far from here, and if you can make it there, the soldiers won't pursue you." She glanced over at Rozaliya. "My friend will make them believe it's haunted."

"She's a witch?" one of the prisoners asked.

"She's an opera singer," Erina replied, smiling at Rozaliya.

Rozaliya returned Erina's smile. "My spells are in my songs."

She and Erina shoved open the back doors to the barn together, and Rozaliya began to sing, without complaint from Erina.

"Tell her that the wrongs against her,
     I'm going to avenge,
That only of killing and death as announcer
     will I return."

Mark Orr

MOURNING MEDUSA

WE BEACHED THE E-BOAT we stole from the small German base on Crete and walked up the hill that was the most prominent feature of the tiny unnamed island. Gestapo chief Heinrich Himmler had let word get out that Hercules' club was supposed to be somewhere in that part of the Aegean Sea, and Major Wilmer Jensen and his elite squad, myself included, set out to snatch it up before the Nazis got their hands on it. Just another in a long series of similar missions.

Bennett scanned the skies for stray recon planes while the major and I stood on the bald knob and surveyed the terrain. There wasn't much to see. If there was a cave in which the club might have been hidden, the entrance wasn't visible from our vantage point. We did notice a tiny peninsula pointing towards the Greek mainland. Major Jensen told Bennett to keep his eyes peeled and crooked a finger at me. We walked down the slope and out onto the spit.

He stopped short and stared at a cluster of statues at Land's End. It was a small group of what looked like German sailors crouching close to the ground with their hands raised before their faces, their features contorted by what looked to me like horrified fascination. I'm no art critic, but they seemed extraordinarily well done, too well done to be stuck on a lonely rock like this. They ought to have been in a museum. I turned and looked at the Major.

He had his gaze locked onto the stone men. He muttered, *"Isla de las Estatuas."*

"Sir?" I asked.

He shook himself and said, "Never mind. There's nothing here. Nothing we need to see. We should move on to the next site."

I followed him back up the slope, wondering what his hurry to get off that island might be. I wanted to know what kind of sculptor leaves a bunch of brand new, brilliantly executed statues out in the wind and rain to slowly erode away.

I knew better than to ask the Major his opinion on that topic. I did forget my place long enough to start to suggest that we should cruise along the shoreline in the e-boat to check the rock faces at the edge of the water for small caves. He cut me off before I got more than a couple of words out. "I told you, there's nothing here you need to see. Let's go."

We collected Bennett and scrambled into the boat. Santos fired up the engine and pointed it across the open water to the next island we were ordered to check.

We got back to Malta before dark. The Major sent us ashore and told us to get a good night's sleep. He was going to stay on the boat and take care of a few chores before hitting the sack.

I woke up after midnight and had to step out to the latrine. On the way back to the barracks, I glanced at the dock. There was no moon that night, so I had to look carefully, then walk over to be sure.

The E-boat was gone.

I woke the others and told them about the statues and the Major's impatience to leave the island, and about the missing boat. We sat up all night, waiting for him to return.

He finally wandered into the common room just after dawn, as disheveled as if he'd wrestled a harem in a Bob Hope movie. The lopsided grin he wore when he sauntered through the door faded away when he saw us arrayed on a semicircle of chairs. He spotted right off that we were waiting patiently for him to tell us a story, as we had waited so many times before. He glared at us and tossed the ancient wooden club he bore into a corner. We stared back silently. Whatever force of personality Major Jensen possessed that usually backed us down had been expended in some strenuous activity during the long night. He plopped into the most comfortable seat in the room with a sigh, poured himself a tall glassful of scotch and lit a Camel. He favored us with the closest thing to a bittersweet smile I ever saw on his face, and began his tale...

* * *

You lot all know I spent time in Nicaragua back in the Twenties, fighting against the Sandinistas with what was then called the Unusual Circumstances Bureau. It didn't become the Supernatural Investigations Bureau until 1937, while I was off dealing with a renegade genie in Madagascar, of all places. My old boss, George Steele, he dreamed that name up one night, and sprang it on us when we got back with the lamp. We liked it, and it stuck.

Ahem. Right, where I was all night. I've told you men about that disastrous mission I undertook in 1927, chasing a Devil's Island escapee through green hell and right onto the stone altar to a forgotten god, and how that damned basalt idol came to life and I lured it over a cliff to shatter on the rocks below. Yes? You were with us when I told that yarn, weren't you, Phillips? Thought so.

Anyhow. I finally returned to our base, one half of me dead, and the other half, close to out of my mind. The boss took one look and decided it was time for me to be sent back to the States. There were things that he had to do to arrange that, so he found me a light duty assignment to keep me occupied until he could get matters worked out. I'd had enough of Central America, so I didn't argue when he posted me on a tiny island off the coast, Isla de las Estatuas, as the first stage on my way home.

Before you translate that, Drago, it means Island of the Statues. The family who once lived in the only halfway habitable structure on the island collected sculptures and set them out here and there all over the estate. Some years after they died off, the Bureau leased the island and used it to track and intercept shipments of supplies to Sandino and his rebels. Since Sandino never got supplies by that route, it was deemed a duty so light as to be virtually nonexistent. Perfect for the human train wreck I'd become.

I didn't mind. I was content to stew in my own

juices, after what had happened in Costa Rica. I barely left the house the first month, and might not have done so then, if I'd not drunk up my whole supply of liquor in the first three weeks. Eventually, I pulled myself together and made a show of watching the channel between me and the mainland at night. There was nothing to see. There never was anything to see except blue water flowing to and from the Caribbean. I gave up after another week and took to exploring my temporary home.

The house was typical of that place and the earlier century in which it was built. I'd set up housekeeping in the intact southernmost wing. The other parts of the house were held up mostly by the hopes and wishes of whatever ghosts still lived there. I never saw one, but my experience has always been that any house from which the tenants vanished mysteriously retains psychic traces of those lost souls.

I decided the tumbledown side must have been the family's favorite, as the bulk of the estate's statuary was congregated outside what was left of its walls. The few pieces on my side of the building were your standard copies of classical figures, down to a plaster Venus de Milo, probably cast within a few years of the original's discovery in 1820. She'd lost some definition over the decades, to put it mildly. Had I not seen the real Venus stumbling around the Louvre looking for her lost arms a few years before, I would likely have not recognized her.

The other pieces on the south side were more of the same, nice in their day but sadly worn by the tropical climate. The statues on the north side, though, were a whole 'nother thing.

It wasn't just that they weren't simply copies of

better known works. They were completely intact, as if they'd been carved only a few years before. And the stone was harder than you'd normally find in that part of the world. I'm not sure how common marble is in Central America, but I somehow doubt the entire supply would have been enough to make up the stone population on the north side of the house.

They looked to be the work of a master sculptor, taking his inspiration from living, moving subjects. The figures seemed to be about to jump off in all directions and run away from you, as if anyone who looked upon them frightened the living daylights out of them.

They weren't classical subjects, either. The figures were clothed in modern garments, or at least not togas and chitons. The ones closest to the house were dressed in finery from the late Eighteenth Century, breeches and cravats on the men, full skirts and mantillas on the women. Farther away, they wore frock coats and top hats and bonnets bedecked with ostrich feathers, each one exquisitely carved. All bore expressions of panic and postures of being on the verge of flight. Even the children seemed terrified. I recall one statue of a boy, maybe five years of age. Whoever carved the rock had so perfectly captured the fear in his tiny features, I wondered what had so perverted the artist's mind to even consider creating such an awful grimace. Even so, the skill with which even so horrific a set of works had been accomplished forced me to respect his artistry, even as I hoped to never meet anyone so warped in their mind, and in their heart.

Each night, after my cursory glance at the channel through which no vessels ever passed, I wandered farther and farther away from the house, admiring the repellent statues that marched in agonized postures into the jungle beyond the overgrown lawn and garden. During the days, I took to clearing vines and brush, discovering more statues the more I worked. Before long, it became an obsession to uncover every figure I could, an obsession that ended one night as I emerged from the forest onto the narrow finger of land that extended out into the calm water and pointed at the mainland.

I remember it as a night of unnatural stillness and quiet. No breeze came in off the sea. No birds called, no monkeys chattered or howled. Even the insects were hushed. You've heard of the calm before the storm. That was it. My barometer had told me to expect a heavy blow, which was why I was so desperate to find the last of the sculptures. If a hurricane were indeed coming, it might take them away. I wanted to see them before they were lost.

It was well that I did. There were two figures there on that last little piece of land. Farthest away from me, at the edge of the peninsula, a man in a frock coat reeled back, arms raised, as if teetering on the edge before plunging into the sea beyond. The other one, nearer, facing the man about to fall, had the shape of a woman with a long flowing skirt. The bodice was sleeveless, and her mass of hair hung down in a solid nimbus around her head.

I paused and scanned the sky. There were no stars, and the light from the moon only penetrated the clouds enough that I could see the outlines of the two figures before me. I shook out a smoke and struck the match on the bark of a tree beside me.

The woman flinched. Her head and left shoulder turned slightly towards me.

"Buenos noches, senorita," I stammered out in my very un-Spanish Hoosier accent.

"You're the American who lives in the big house on the hill," she responded in English. Her accent was strange, one I had never heard before. Her voice was soft as silk lingerie falling onto a carpeted floor, and as seductive. It was a purr that drew one to it, but I'd been purred at by beings whose embrace did not match up with the delights promised. You've heard one or two of those tales.

"Sorry to disturb you," I said without moving any closer to her. "I was under the impression there was no one else living on the island."

She moved gracefully to her right a few steps and sank down onto a stone bench that must have been installed back when the family who built the house first moved in. She never turned completely towards me, but kept her gaze on the frozen man and the sea beyond. "I would prefer to keep my presence here a secret, if you don't mind."

"I don't mind a bit," I said. "Have you been here long?"

"Oh, so very long," she sighed. "It seems like centuries."

A little moonlight came through just then, enough that I could see that her hair was arranged in thick braids all over her head, perhaps shoulder length. They fluttered a bit as I stood there, and I had a sudden urge to rush forward and see her face.

I squelched that impulse. She clearly did not want to be disturbed, so I took my leave of her.

A boat arrived the next day just before noon, bearing supplies. I resisted the temptation to ask about my mysterious cohabitant, while the crew carried cases up the hill to my headquarters.

"You should hunker down," the captain told me. "We're expecting a big storm tomorrow, maybe the day after. We won't be able to reach you. You're on your own."

I told him I understood, and thanked him for the whiskey. They left just before sunset. I hurried out through the jungle and reached the peninsula just as it got very dark. The moon was still shrouded, but I saw her standing where she had been before. I paused and admired her figure, outlined as it was against the luminescence of the water. It was more curvaceous than I had noticed the previous night, but I wasn't there to flirt. Not entirely, anyhow.

"Excuse me," I said to her back.

"Yes?" she said without turning.

"There's a storm coming."

She sighed, the kind of sigh that makes a man want to take a woman into his arms. I held back, though. As I said, experience had even then instilled in me a wariness of such enticements.

"Yes," she said at length. "There is a storm coming. One of so many I've lived through. I suspect I shall live through this one, too."

"If you need a place to ride it out," I said, "There's plenty of room at the house."

"Ride it out," she said, as if she were turning the phrase over in her mind, examining it, figuring it out. "Thank you, but I have a place to go to. I will be quite safe."

I glanced at the sky. The wind suddenly came up. Her long skirt fluttered, although her hair was still.

"If you change your mind," I said, backing away, "you know where to find me."

"Yes, I do."

I left her there and made it back to the house before the first squall line arrived.

I was unable to leave the cellar for three days. When I emerged, the house was covered in palm fronds, but as far as I could tell, intact. Some of the nearer statues were badly damaged, however. One or two were gone altogether. I spent the day clearing debris away from the doors and walkway I had to use to get out and about.

It was full dark when I made my way to the only spot on the island where I thought I might find my mysterious neighbor. The air was still and almost as sultry as it was on the night of our first meeting. The moon was unobscured, a barely visible crescent among a myriad of stars. In what light it shed, I saw her standing there on the spit, a dark figure outlined in faint white. She stared out at the water, looking through the place where the statue of the falling man had been a few days before.

"Your friend seems to have taken a powder," I said at her back.

I expected to hear sadness in her voice, but there was a lightness in it I had not heard before. She didn't exactly laugh, but I imagined there was a smile on her face.

"I have never heard that expression," she said, "but I think I understand the sentiment. Yes, he has left me quite alone out here."

"The cad," I said.

Her braids swayed in the dim light as she started to turn towards me. She didn't finish the movement.

"Perhaps he was jealous of my new suitor," she purred. She turned her head back around to face the sea.

"A suitor should know the name of the object of his affections," I said.

She took a moment to answer. "You may call me Emma."

I gave her my name. She admitted she was happy to know me. She sat again, her back still to me. I found a rock behind me to plant myself on. I asked her where she was from.

She raised a long arm towards the east. "Very far, that direction," she said, then pointed north. "And you are from there."

I confessed to that truth.

"I would have liked to have visited America. The last family who lived here had magazines with pictures from America in them. They...left them here when they went away. I still look at them."

"I'd love to show you my country," I said. "It's a pretty impressive place."

She sighed, deeper and with a heavier weight of melancholy than I had ever heard before, from her or anyone else. "I wish you could. That Statue of Liberty must be something to behold."

"I would think you'd be sick to death of statues," I said.

Her back stiffened, and her braids seem to flare out on her head. "I am," she said, more coldly than she had spoken up to that point.

I began to apologize, but she cut me off. "No, I am the one who should be sorry. You could not know, and you have been nothing but a complete gentleman since we first met. You did not deserve to be spoken to in that manner." Her back, and her hair, relaxed again.

When the silence grew uncomfortable, I cleared my

throat and said, "I got in some interesting cases of preserved foods just before the storm hit. If you're hungry, I'd be happy to exercise my skill at opening cans and heating the contents in what's left of the kitchen up there."

She raised her arms to indicate the jungle around us. "My wants are more than met by the natural world. Fruits, berries and nuts fill my needs nicely. But I thank you for your kindness."

"Well, then," I said as I stood. "I'll take my leave of you. I've had a long, busy day, and expect another one tomorrow. If you need anything, you know where to find me."

"I do," she purred as I turned away from her.

And so she did. Something woke me late that night, a slight noise, or a scent, or a feeling I cannot attribute to any of the regular array of senses. I sat up in my bed and looked to the doors that opened onto the patio beyond. A female form cast a shadow into the room, lit from behind by the dim light from the waning moon. The chiaroscuro figure swayed gently in the breeze.

I reached out and pulled aside the mosquito netting. She walked towards me, and stood over me a long moment. She had piled her hair up on top of her head and wound a turban around it. She wore nothing else. I moved over, and she slid into the bed beside me.

I'm far too much of a gentleman to describe the events of that night. I'm sure you reprobates can fill in the picture in your own feverish minds. I will only say that she never let me disturb the turban she wore on her head. I was allowed to explore her face and her body with my hands, and I found them as soft and smooth and as perfectly shaped as I've ever known a woman's form and features to be. I came up with a pretty good idea of what she looked like, and that was more than enough for me.

We lay there afterwards, basking in each other's warmth. I raised a hand to caress her cheek, and something stung my hand. She sat up and tucked a loose strand back under the turban while I clutched the wound.

It burned like a coal that falls off the end of a cigarette, but deeper, down into the soft tissues. She grabbed my hand and clamped her mouth over the sore spot. She sucked at it, and my head reeled. I grew faint, and remember nothing else until just before dawn.

I awoke and staggered out of my room and into the darkness outside. I stumbled down the path to the spit where we'd met before. I fell across the stone bench, half-conscious, and looked to the east as the light of the sun first colored the sea at the horizon. There was a boat out there on the water, a small craft with a white hull and a single triangular sail. I got to my feet and found the path down to the beach. Four new statues had appeared in the sand, sculptures of armed men charging forward like an invading force. I ran between them to the edge of the surf, and stared at the boat.

A lone figure stood in the stern. Emma. She lifted an arm to wave at me. Her hair writhed around her head. I thought it must have been ruffled by the breeze that filled the sail, forcing the boat farther out to sea. I waved back, then collapsed into the sand.

I came to several days later, in a hospital tent at our camp on the mainland. My boss came and sat by my bed to take my report.

"I found this note in your room," Steele said when I'd finished. He held it up and adjusted his glasses. He cleared his throat. "'Thank you for your courtesy,'" he read. "'It has been so many years since a man was kind to me. I am sorry our evening did not end well. The bite you received on your hand will not be fatal, although you will take some time to recover. The same cannot be said of most of the men I have encountered in the course of my very long and very unfortunate life. I wish I could stay with you and greet the dawn the way lovers should, but you would not like what you saw in the light of day.'"

"Too bad," I said. "I touched her face, explored it with my fingertips. As near as I could tell, she was the most beautiful woman I have ever been with."

He shrugged and continued reading. "'I walked down to our usual meeting place a few moments ago. I saw a boat sailing towards us. I fear you have enemies coming to hurt you. I will not let that happen. I will deal with this intrusion, and then I will move on to some other place where the world can be protected from my curse. I hope you think of me fondly from time to time, and know that not all monsters are as bad as people think.'"

He lowered the paper. "What do you think she meant by that?" he asked.

I didn't answer.

He pulled a photograph from inside his jacket and handed it to me. "Is that the boat she was in?"

I took the picture and stared at it. A triangular sail lay on the water, the port side of a whitewashed hull showing below the boom.

"We found it capsized over a hundred miles out," he said, "after a squall passed through that part of the Caribbean and on across the Leeward Islands. There were no signs of a survivor, and there was no land anywhere around it. She must have drowned."

"Or wants us to think she has," I said. I handed the photograph back to him. "Maybe it's best if we do."

"Those four statues on the beach," he said. "They weren't there when you arrived on the island."

"No, they weren't," I responded.

"How do you think they got there?"

"What bit my hand?" I asked.

He leaned back in the chair. "The doctor says it was a small venomous snake. He found traces of a neurotoxin, like a cobra's, but someone had sucked most of it out."

"I guess I must have loosened her turban," I said. "Just a little. Just enough."

Steele sat a long time before nodding and leaning forward. He patted me on the shoulder. "You'll be back home in a few days. I've arranged for you to recuperate at my place in Tennessee." He stood. "You're a lucky man, to have survived an encounter with her. I think we both have a good idea who that was. None of my dates ever had snakes for hair."

I gave him the best grin I could muster. "Luck is a family trait."

He nodded and walked away. I let the grin fade. I calculated that I might not be able to rely on the Old Jensen Luck to save me if I ever ran into her again. Which was a distinct possibility, given my chosen profession.

It's not that I actively went looking for her, you understand. That would be foolhardy. But I did keep my eye out for any reports of suspicious statuary turning up in unexpected places. There were no such reports, as far as I have been able to discover, for a very long time. Until yesterday.

I let myself think that Emma did drown in the sea.

I hated to think so, but I had no reason to disbelieve it. I always considered it to be a terrible shame, though. Monster or not, she did me a good turn, and deserved better than to end three thousand years of misery and horror so alone, and forgotten.

*   *   *

The Major stubbed out his last smoke and rubbed his eyes. He drained his glass and told us he was going to hit the hay.

"No wonder you wanted us off that island," I said before he could get out of his seat.

"Believe it or not, you men do have some small useful role to play in winning this war. I couldn't risk losing even one of you."

"We appreciate that," Santos said.

"I see you found the club," Bennett pointed out.

The Major eyed the artifact. "Yes, I did. Last night."

"On the same island you chased us off of as fast as you could." I said. "You went back there. You found it, and you found your Emma."

He gave me a long stare before answering. "Let's just say I'm no longer mourning her."

"And you're much too much of a gentleman to explain what you were up to for most of the night," I pointed out.

"I spent a good portion of it tracking down that blasted stick you bums were too lazy to fetch for yourselves," the Major growled. "Whatever else I might have done has been on my own time and none of your damned business."

He cleared his throat and stood. "The plane for Tibet leaves at 1800 hours," he said. "Get your cold-weather gear packed, then catch a few winks. We've got a lot of work to do once we get there. Occult artifacts don't find themselves."

We got to our feet and pointed our toes in the direction of our bunks. We were almost to the door when Bennett turned and said, "Wait a minute. Venus de Milo did what?"

Drago yawned and stretched. "Wandered around the Louvre, looking for her arms. That's what he said, anyway."

"How did she manage that?" Santos asked.

The Major shook his head and shoved us out of the room. "Another tale, boys. For another time."

Anya Ow

GARUDA

MAY LEE FOLDED HER HANDS over her shorn scalp and made herself small in the undergrowth. The annoying, itchy samfu that she wore now felt like a blessing. The dark dyed fabric hid her from the dappled sunlight that filtered past the jungle canopy. Above the hidden women and girls, the sky was screaming.

The Japanese planes had already done their sweep. Earlier in the war, it had been possible to watch dogfights in the air from clearings near the camp. The roar of planes and the rat-tat-tat of their guns had been common, along with the occasional blast from a bomb. The metallic shrieks as the tengu darted through the sky in graceful sweeps, the aerial troops more agile than any British plane. They'd looked like silver sparrows harrying clumsy pigeons with needles. May Lee had once thought them beautiful.

She scorned her younger self as the tengu cut

across the cloudy sky in lazy loops. Encased in their silver flight suits, with their huge black wings outstretched and their dog-like red masks on their faces, the tengu troops looked nothing human. They had their bayonets hugged close, their feet stretched stiffly behind them. Lightning forked restlessly over their wings from canisters strapped to their backs, somehow keeping them aloft as they made another balletic loop over the trees. Searching.

Something crawled over May Lee's ankle. She didn't dare to look, biting on the inside of her cheek to keep herself from crying out. Auntie Chia was curled under the next bush, her broad back facing May Lee. Annie was somewhere behind May Lee. She was sobbing softly. Annie always cried when they had to hide. Whenever one of the tengu passed overhead, May Lee resented her cousin for the noise she made. May Lee would always feel ashamed of her resentment afterwards, during the walk back to camp. It was hard to remember shame now, pressed to the soil and mud with her hands clawed into her shaved scalp.

May Lee's bladder was starting to ache by the time the tengu grew bored of sweeping the area and flew away. She started to count to one thousand in her head. When May Lee reached five hundred and four, Auntie Chia let out a grunt and got to her feet, grumbling to herself in Hakka. May Lee checked her leg. Large black ants were crawling over her ankle, investigating her shoe. Shaking them off, May Lee stood up and stretched. Around her, the scattered women and children were rising out of bushes and ferns. The jungle stayed breathless for a few heartbeats longer before the cicadas started to sing.

As Auntie Chia started her headcount, May Lee

sidled over to Annie. "Are you all right?" May Lee whispered in Cantonese, already ashamed.

Annie nodded, rubbing her eyes. She was new to Senai—her family had fled up into Malaya from Singapore when the British had surrendered. "I'm fine," Annie said. Her Cantonese was rusty, interspersed with English words. She let May Lee pull her to her feet, shaking so violently that May Lee had to steady her with a hand on her shoulder. "That's the first time I've seen Raijin tech so close."

"Raijin?"

"The tengu flight suits, the Susanoo motherships, they're Raijin tech. Chthonic lightning technology."

"Oh," May Lee said.

Annie's branch of the family had some money —she had been sent to an English school in Singapore before the war. It had scarred her in unexpected ways. The language of the world that it had equipped her with was incomprehensible to almost everyone in the camp. She had learned English when everyone in the camp spoke Malay or Chinese dialects. Worse, it had mired her in practical lies about reality. As Annie brushed herself down, she said, "I still can't believe that the British lost Singapore to soldiers on bicycles. They used to make us sing 'Britannia Rules the Waves' in school."

May Lee nodded. News that the British had lost Singapore had come as a crushing disappointment. When the Allied forces had retreated past the refugee camp, they'd abandoned guns and supplies. "I saw them pass." The guns were now buried under the house in the camp that was shared by the Teck and Tan families.

"Why do we hide here, though? The jungle's deeper

past there." Annie pointed. May Lee didn't have to look. She could hear the small stream behind her, the rocky brook that marked the boundary of their flight.

"We'll get lost," May Lee said.

"We've been up and down here every few days."

May Lee scowled. She'd never questioned why this section of the forest had been chosen as a hiding spot. "We've always been OK here."

Auntie Chia finished her headcount and glanced over before Annie could reply. "We don't go further than the stream," she told Annie as she glanced over her shoulder. "Too far down that way and the garuda will get you."

Annie stared at her. "Garuda? A giant magic bird? Auntie, I'm no longer a baby."

Auntie Chia was unimpressed. "We just watched men fly across the sky on wings of lightning. What's so hard to believe about a magic bird?"

"That's *technology*," Annie said. She shot the deep jungle a doubtful look. "If the garuda's there, why doesn't it fly out and eat the Japanese? The tengu and the planes aren't exactly quiet."

"The war's none of its business," Auntie Chia said. She started chivvying people away from the stream. "Come, come. Once we get home, I'll make everyone some *tau hway*."

The promise of a treat had the desired effect. Even Annie brightened up as they picked their way through the dense ferns to begin the hours-long trek back to the refugee camp, monsters and monster birds forgotten.

* * *

Auntie Chia was a one-woman bean curd machine. In between chores, May Lee loved watching her work.

First, she would grind pre-soaked soybeans with a granite grinder, rotating the sectioned top with an attached wooden pole as she hummed tunelessly. The ground soya would be sieved through a worn cloth, the milk boiled with additives. The resulting curd was squeezed through more cloth, weighted on top with rocks to remove the water. The resulting cake, *tau hway,* was a treat when eaten with syrup. May Lee had watched the process over a hundred times now and it was still magic. No Raijin tech required.

She sat with Annie, each of them savouring a small bowl. The food in camp was rationed, but according to Annie, they were better off than most. Sweet potatoes and vegetables were grown in between the rows of rubber trees. The rubber estate was now a camp that held hundreds of people. The grand old house that sprawled in the centre of the compound had been sectioned off into little rooms. The people who would have usually occupied the leftmost wing of the house had been temporarily turned out and had taken shelter under the rubber trees. The owner of the estate, their uncle, was having a private meeting with a few fighters from the Malayan resistance. Annie had once asked her uncle why nobody else was allowed in during these meetings. Safer that way, he'd said, looking tired. He always looked tired nowadays.

"Do you think the garuda is real?" Annie asked.

"If Auntie Chia says it's real, it's real," May Lee said. She'd been hoping for a glimpse of the visitors but had arrived too late from fieldwork.

"If it's anything like the stories, it'd easily be able to take on the tengu," Annie said.

"Maybe it doesn't think it's worth the trouble. Maybe it's asleep." May Lee's experience of giant magical creatures was spotty at best. "The animals in the jungle have been shy, and I don't blame them." With refugees pouring into the jungle, animals had learned to fear their noisy new predators.

"Raja said that they killed and ate a boar the other day," Annie said. Raja was the leader of the local group of resistance fighters.

May Lee perked up. "You talked to him? When?"

"I was on sweeping duty in the Big House when they showed up," Annie said.

"Wow," May Lee said. Annie pulled a face. May Lee scowled at her. "What? You don't like him?"

"He's just here to ask for money again. Mama says they've been bleeding money from Uncle Sen for a while. And for what?" Annie gestured up at the sky. "The tengu, the Japanese, they're still everywhere. We have to hide every few days because they're here looking for Raja and the others. Worse, if the Japanese ever find out that Uncle Sen was funding them? They'd kill us all."

"Everyone? No lah. That time when the Japanese came to inspect the camp, Teck said that they were pretty friendly. Showed him and the other boys their samurai swords. The Taiwanese translator with them said they missed their families back home."

Annie let out a snort. "And where were we?"

"Hiding?"

"Why were we hiding?"

"Because Auntie Alice said they'd do bad things to us if we got caught," May Lee said. The threat had been left deliberately murky. May Lee had felt the keen injustice of having had to spend several hot hours trekking through jungle and back, while the boys her age had gotten to look at samurai swords. She still didn't entirely understand why only the women and girls had to hide whenever the Japanese were flying overhead drills or conducting inspections. They were just searching for the Malayan resistance or for enemy soldiers, weren't they? That had nothing to do with May Lee.

"Exactly," Annie said darkly. She started to say more but fell silent as someone walked over briskly from the Big House. It was Raja. He was a compact man with a thick moustache and a friendly, devil-may-care grin. He had a knife tucked into his belt, the sewn-on pockets just over the knees of his pants bulging and heavy.

"Ahhh. Annie, May Lee. And my favourite person, Miss Chia." Raja winked at Auntie Chia, who giggled.

"You're a bad person, always coming around and making trouble," Auntie Chia said. She passed Raja a bowl of *tau hway* without being asked, laughing as he complimented her in florid terms before strolling over to sit on the grass beside Annie.

"Is it true that the Japanese do bad things to girls?" May Lee asked.

Raja's grin faded. He held the bowl carefully in his hands and looked over at Auntie Chia, who had wandered off to inspect the grinder. "Yes. What they did to Nanjing...Hai, no need to talk about Nanjing. I've seen what they do. The 'comfort houses' in Singapore—" He cut himself off with a grimace. "That's why you two should listen to your aunties and hide when you have to."

"Comfort houses?" May Lee asked. That didn't sound too scary.

Raja looked embarrassed. "Forget that I told you that. I pray to the Gods that you'll never have to know."

"How's the resistance going?" Annie asked. She ignored May Lee's warning glance.

"Not too bad, not too bad," Raja said. He smiled at Annie. "The less you know the better. Just in case."

"Isn't it already too late? If the Japanese find out Uncle Sen is helping you, they'll come here and kill all of us," Annie said.

"*Annie,*" May Lee protested.

"No, no. She's right," Raja said. He patted Annie on the shoulder. "We're careful. Don't worry."

"What if we used a weapon that can't be traced to anyone?" Annie asked. She lowered her voice. "A weapon so powerful that it could get rid of the tengu around here. Maybe chase away all the Japanese. Then we could all go home. I could go back to Singapore."

"Well," Raja said, with a wry smile, "it depends on the weapon. You're talking about the bomb? One of the runaway POWs we found mentioned something. A bomb so big, it could end the war."

"Really? Something like that exists? Why are we still fighting then?" May Lee demanded.

"I've seen what a small bomb can do. It doesn't care what it hurts. Kids, women, everyone. A big bomb...a very big bomb?" Raja shuddered. "I hope they find another way."

Annie looked away at the jungle, pensive.

* * *

May Lee only realized that Annie was missing when she didn't hear her sobbing. She looked around wildly and saw the trail of broken leaves and dirt leading toward the stream. May Lee clenched her fingertips into her arms as the tengu shrilled overhead.

What if Annie fell into the water and drowned? She couldn't swim. May Lee crawled after the trail, praying under her breath.

Annie hadn't gotten far. She was on her feet on the opposite bank of the stream, brushing the dirt from her knees. "Annie!" May Lee hissed.

"Go back," Annie said. Her smeared face was set in unfathomable determination. "I'm going to look for the garuda."

"You'd get lost! Or you'd get caught by the tengu. Eaten by tigers and snakes."

"I won't. The jungle's thicker past the brook and the animals are all in hiding." Annie pushed ferns out of her way as she walked deeper into the jungle.

"Annie!" May Lee jumped to her feet. She crossed the stream awkwardly, canvas shoes slipping over rocks. "You don't even think garudas are real. Where are you going to go?"

"I talked to Raja and the hunters. There's a part of the jungle that they avoid. Even the tigers avoid it. The old temple with the golden statue."

"Anything golden around here would have been stolen long ago," May Lee said.

"It's still there. Has to be because there's something there. It isn't that far from here. I'll be back in the camp before night. Go back."

May Lee shook her head. "Auntie Chia will scold me if I go back without you. If it's not far, we'll both go. Quickly."

Annie nodded. They stumbled through the jungle, pushing their way past ferns and climbing over roots and fallen branches. Their shoes squelched underfoot, their samfu sticking to their backs from the humidity and excitement. Occasionally, a particularly loud whine from overhead would send them ducking against a tree, but as they walked deeper and deeper into the jungle, it grew harder and harder to see the tengu. The jungle was growing unnaturally dense, unnaturally still. May Lee usually had a good eye for picking out bugs, birds, and other wildlife. Here she saw nothing, and she doubted it was because of the patrols.

"Feel that," Annie whispered.

May Lee flinched, then had to bite down on her lip to stifle a yelp as Annie pressed a hand to her arm. Her fingertips were freezing cold. May Lee touched her own hands to her neck. Now that she wasn't concentrating on hiding, it grew obvious that the jungle around them was growing colder. Less humid. "Magic?" May Lee mouthed. Annie frowned and kept walking. They could barely see where they were going. It felt like the jungle itself was trying to push them back. The air around them was growing crisper, easier and easier to breathe.

Annie sniffed. There was a strange smell thickening around them, a rain-smell. She snapped her fingers and yelped as a spark of light danced from her fingertips.

"How did you...?" May Lee snapped her fingers. The same thing happened. She gawked.

"Chthonic breach," Annie said, grinning broadly. "We read about it in school. The Japanese, the British, the Americans, they drain them for energy. Raijin tech's the most advanced of the lot, but the principle's the same."

"Stealing from the underworld. Auntie Chia says it's cursed." May Lee said.

Annie looked briefly annoyed. "That's just superstition. It's not the underworld, it's another dimension. One with different rules. That's how the tengu can fly, how Mjolner weaponry can breach tanks. It's all science."

"Looks like both," May Lee said. She snapped her fingers again and smiled at the spark. "It's beautiful. It's not dangerous?"

"Not if we don't stay that long. C'mon. We're close. The colder it gets, the closer we are. The 'magic bird' will probably be at the centre of the phenomenon."

"You know a lot," May Lee said enviously, as she followed Annie into the cold.

"My dad's an engineer. He had a lot of books in the house in Singapore," Annie said.

"He's in America now, isn't he?" May Lee couldn't even imagine what it would be like to leave Senai, let alone go all the way across the world.

Annie nodded grimly. "Working on a secret project. He wouldn't say what. Work, work. It's all he does. He was working when mum got sick and died."

"Working on something important? The thing that can end the war? That Raja mentioned?"

"I don't think so," Annie said, after a pause. "He hates weapons."

"What, everything? Even knives?"

"Everything." Annie rolled her eyes. "It's people I hate. The Japanese. The British. Everyone involved in this awful war." Anger blazed so hotly from Annie that it was hard to reconcile this furious, snarling child with the girl who had sobbed behind May Lee in the bushes.

"I don't hate anyone," May Lee said. Even the years of fear and privation hadn't managed to make her hate.

"I know." Annie stumbled over a root. She batted away May Lee's hands when May Lee tried to steady her, and they kept walking in silence.

*   *   *

The stone temple rose out of the ferns as a ruin. Moss and ferns had long overgrown the blocky walls. It was smaller than the latrines back in the camp and held only a weathered old idol that was about May Lee's height. It had probably been golden once. The paint had flaked off everything but parts of the scalp.

"Someone knew this place was special," Annie said as she walked over to the temple. "It's coldest here, where the temple is. The centre of the breach."

"You're sure it's not dangerous," May Lee said.

"Nothing's here." Annie walked around the temple slowly, staring at the ground. "Help me look for tracks. Bird tracks."

"Won't a bird fly?" May Lee asked, but Annie was already walking away.

Instead of following her, May Lee stepped slowly into the temple for a closer look at the statue. She couldn't tell whether it had once meant to be of a man or of a creature. It had a hooked nose or beak, and a lumpy back. She touched her fingertips to the gold paint. The temperature plunged. May Lee yelped and stumbled back, landing on her butt on the grass.

"May Lee!" Annie darted back around the temple. She looked up and gawked.

A colourful bird sat on the crown of the statue. It was a huge parrot, taller than the statue, brilliantly colourful. Its chest was a burnished orange, its head and crest blue and yellow, its wings every colour of the rainbow. It tilted its head as it studied them both with golden eyes.

"That...doesn't look like a garuda," May Lee said shakily.

The bird fluffed its wings, as though indignant.

"Not a garuda, no," it said in a deep, rasping voice. "I'm a Bayan. Well? What do you humans want?"

Shocked, both girls stared at the bird. "You speak," May Lee said.

"You speak *Cantonese*," Annie said.

The Bayan shifted its weight on its perch. "I speak whatever language I want. Well?"

Annie cleared her throat a few times. "O Great and Wise Bayan—"

"Someone's been reading a lot of stories. Get on with it, child. I don't like the smell of your world, and it's very noisy."

Annie blushed. "Erm. I'll like to know where the garuda bird is, please."

"That's an easy one. Nowhere," the Bayan said.

Annie sagged. "It doesn't exist?" May Lee asked, disappointed.

The Bayan eyeballed her. "I didn't say that."

"Where do we find it? Please," May Lee said, "and thank you."

"It is not found," the Bayan said, "it finds." As May Lee scrunched her face up in frustration, the bird said kindly, "Girl, what do you want?"

"Me? Uh. Peace, I guess," May Lee said. She winced at another whine in the air, far away as sounded. "Can you do that?"

"You already have it," the Bayan said, cocking its head. "Your camp is tolerated. You have shelter and enough to eat. You live in peace enough, compared to many others of your kind."

"Not really," May Lee said, though under the Bayan's withering stare the rest of her retort withered unsaid.

Annie stepped forward, hands clenched. "I want to get rid of the tengu. I want to drive the Japanese soldiers away from here."

"Your wish and your friend's wish are incompatible," the Bayan said.

"They're the same," Annie shot back.

"You want vengeance," said the Bayan.

"I want justice," Annie said. Her eyes blazed. "I want them gone. I want to go home."

"Now that I understand. What will you trade?" asked the Bayan.

"Annie," May Lee warned.

Annie ignored her. "What do you want? My soul?"

"There's no such thing." The Bayan chuckled. "I'll settle for your memory. Of everything that you were, and are, and will be."

"Done," Annie said.

"*Annie.*" May Lee reached for Annie's wrist, but Annie shrugged her off.

"Step outside, child," said the Bayan. It stretched out its wings, arcing them over the crumbling stone.

Annie walked out of the temple. May Lee tried to follow but stumbled and fell on her knees at the doorway. As she looked up, she clapped her hands to her mouth. Annie was starting to burn as she walked. Great sheets of lightning leapt from her shoulders, stretching higher and higher. Annie started to rise into the air, her arms outstretched, her knees pressed together, rising higher and higher until she became a small blot at the heart of a star. Annie did not scream as she became the garuda. She beat her new wings, taking herself higher over the forest, higher into the clouds. Only then did she let out a ringing cry, a shriek of joyous challenge. The garuda charged.

The tengu milled around at first, startled by the sudden attack, the novel enemy. They rallied quickly as the garuda closed in, tiny specks that fell into formation and darted in to harry at the garuda with their rifles. The garuda twisted in the air and spread its wings. Lightning sprang from the backs of the tengu, leaping towards the garuda. It swallowed the offering whole.

As it ate the lightning, the bird grew bigger, brighter. It shrieked again as the tengu fell from the sky. Taking itself in a slow circuit over the jungle, the garuda looked briefly in May Lee's direction. Its great wings broke the air as it circled away, taking itself away from the forest, towards the sea.

The Bayan began to laugh. May Lee turned. The bird was starting to fade. "Run, little girl," the Bayan said. Its wings and feet were already translucent. "The friends of the people she killed will return in force. They'd want blood. I said that your wish and your friend's wish were incompatible."

"What friend?" May Lee asked, but the Bayan was gone. May Lee stared at the empty temple in confusion. Why was she here? Turning away, May Lee broke into a brisk jog as she headed back to where Auntie Chia and the others were still hiding. There was going to be trouble.

★★★★ CURIOSITIES ★★★★

CANTEEN

— ✦✦✦ — *with Anya Ow* — ✦✦✦ —

and Andrew McCurdy

Andrew: Hi Anya. I'd like to start by thanking you for agreeing to meet me in the Curiosities Canteen. We have been including these author interviews since the second issue and it has become one of my favourite sections.

Anya: Thanks for having me. And for giving my story a home!

Andrew: Without giving away the ending can you say a bit about your story, "Garuda," included in this collection.

Anya: "Garuda" is about two young girls, May Lee and Annie, as they live through their days in a refugee camp in a forest in Malaysia during the Japanese Occupation. They hear stories of a mythical bird in the forest, and Annie decides to look for it, hoping that it might drive the Japanese soldiers away.

Andrew: Many of our readers will be unfamiliar with the mythological background of the creature in your story. Would you be able to share how you first learned of the Garuda?

Anya: Garuda is the name of the national airline of Indonesia–that's most likely how I first heard of the name. I can't really pinpoint exactly when I realized that the airline took its name from a mythical creature, but I've always been interested in Asian myths and mythological creatures. The Garuda is a divine bird or bird-like creature in Jain, Hindu, and Buddhist myths.

Andrew: Because of family history, when I think of the war, I think of the cold North Atlantic, escape stories, and naval battles. How do you picture it?

Anya: Hitler, the atomic bomb, and the Japanese Occupation of Singapore. That's very much how World War II was taught to me in Singapore when I was in second-ary school (high school). Everyone learns that the British tried to create Fortress Singapore in WWII, that the eventual surrender was a surprise to everyone—it was the largest surrender of British forces in history. I used to picture severed heads displayed on the street, the mass graves, able-bodied men rounded up and shot in the sea. That was all my grandmother ever mentioned to me about the war, though the language barrier didn't help. She spoke no English and understood Mandarin, I speak shaky Mandarin and understand Cantonese and some Hakka.

A few years ago, my uncle Linus decided prior to his 80th birthday to write a memoir in English, a family-only book about our family history. Family members contributed photographs and stories, and helped with editing, while I worked on the typesetting and design of the book. It was this memoir that held the complete story of my family's experience of surviving the war, drawn from his memories of those years as a boy. Now when I think of WWII, I think of women trying to hide in the forests, of a boy watching planes fighting overhead.

Andrew: Tell me about some of your other writing.

Anya: My short story, "Eight-step Kōan" (in *Sword and Sonnet*), was shortlisted for this year's Aurealis Awards, and "Big Mother" (*Strange Horizons*) is in 2019's *Year's Best Dark Fantasy and Horror*. "Eight-step Kōan" is very much a story about family and inherited consequences, "Big Mother" about childhood in liminal spaces in Singapore. Over the years, I've tried to write more stories that have settings and/or characters that are more centered on who I am and where I'm from.

Andrew: Are you working on anything at the moment?

Anya: I'm always working on something, though it might not get anywhere. Other than the occasional short story, at present I'm writing the sequel to *The Firebird's Tale*, my first book. Going back and reading older work is always a strange feeling, let alone rereading repeatedly to prep for the sequel. On one hand, I'm glad to see I've improved over the years as a writer (and hopefully as a person), on the other hand, I wish I could go into the devices/books of everyone who bought a copy to edit all the mistakes I now see.

Andrew: Do you have a specific writing routine or practices you follow?

Anya: I'm a pure pantser/organic writer... so no, I sit down with my cats and a cup of tea and write when I have the time. If I'm not writing, I'm usually trying to read through my endless to-read list or longform articles.

Andrew: What do you look for in feedback from your readers?

Anya: I don't often get reader feedback so it's a nice surprise to get the occasional email or message online. I don't think I look for anything in particular. It's a relief to hear from people and know that they liked my work.

Andrew: What do you like to read for pleasure, are there specific genres, and who are some authors that appeal to you?

Anya: I mostly read science fiction and fantasy books, with occasional nonfiction, and longform journalism. For SF&F, I love books with non-standard settings with great world-building and characters. My fave authors include N.K. Jemisin, S.A. Chakraborty, and Liu Cixin. For journalism, Ben Taub's work for *The New Yorker* is great. That being said, the book that had the most impact on me so far this year was nonfiction—David Wallace-Wells' *The Uninhabitable Earth*. It's an incredible book.

Andrew: A friend of mine was recently telling me about N. K. Jemisin. She is a prolific writer. Where would you recommend a new reader start with her work?

Anya: I always try and push people to read *The Fifth Season*, if only because that's the book that made me fall in love with her work. It's wildly imaginative contemp-orary fantasy, beautifully written, and the trilogy is finished. She does also have some short stories available online though, if people just want to read a taster and try out her style—like "The City Born Great."

Andrew: This next one comes from my ten years as a college professor: what question were you prepared to answer but was not covered in this interview. 3 points for the question; 2 points for the answer.

Anya: I get asked variants of this one often: "Why did you switch from law to advertising?" Ans: People who ask me why I stopped working as a lawyer have never worked as a lawyer.

Andrew: That's great, thanks for joining us in the Curiosities Canteen. Don't worry about the drinks, Kevin's picking up the tab. It was a pleasure reading your story. Cheers.

Anya: Cheers!

Adrian Chamberlin

Warpigs

THERE WAS BLOOD ON THE SNOW.

Oberstleutnant Hartmann leaned forward, one hand held over his eyes to block out the bright midwinter sun that had turned the frozen liquid to a gleaming plate of crimson.

SS Major Werther had his hands inside his great coat, tapping his boot heels on the frozen ground. Whether it was from impatience or the biting cold, Hartmann neither knew nor cared. The youngster had much to learn, and he was in no hurry to rush Werther's education.

The frozen blood formed a metre-wide circular pool on a flattened piece of earth. Hartmann had the insane thought that if he pressed his boot on it, the pool would crack and give way beneath him, hurling him into icy fathoms of chilled blood.

After a few moments of closer inspection he raised

his head and stared at the hilly terrain that stretched beyond the clearing the two men stood in. Yesterday's snowfall had frozen solid overnight, a shroud for the skeletal trees and rocky ground of the Breton landscape. The bright sunlight seemed a bad joke, in very poor taste. Behind them, the black Mercedes staff car idled gently, sending plumes of white exhaust into the unnaturally blue sky.

"It's human," he said softly without facing his subordinate. "One of your men, Major."

"Bastard partisans!" Werther's voice was as dry and cold as the afternoon air. "I told you the *Maquisards* are operating here. The village—"

"I don't think so, Major." Hartmann's words were smooth and mellifluous, but the softness of his voice did not hint at any weakness. Few men rise to the rank of Lieutenant-Colonel in the Wehrmacht with anything less than iron will. It was this steel that had saved him and his men on countless engagements on the Eastern Front and had earned him the Iron Cross. A scar running the length of his right thigh was a small price to pay for the survival of his men, he had said to the Führer when the medal was presented to him.

But the scar was not the result of an engagement with the Bolsheviks. And that battle on the banks of the Volga had been fought for survival, not the glory of the Reich. Hitler did not know the full details, which was just as well. Even the mad Austrian would have had difficulty believing what had faced Hartmann that day, or how he had survived.

Werther stared at him, his fat lips pursed in an adolescent pout. Hartmann shook his head in disgust. The SS major was in his early twenties, scarcely more than a boy. Despite his rank he had yet to see real combat, unlike Hartmann, who still had vivid memories of serving in the Great War when he was younger than the major was now.

A few easy postings in Paris, gathering intelligence for the Gestapo was the sum total of his experience. Interrogating suspected SOE operatives on the fifth floor of 84 Avenue Foch was not what Hartmann classed as active military service.

"Why not, *Oberstleutnant?*" The title was sneered, an insult. "Share your wisdom, please."

Hartmann sighed heavily and removed his *schirm-mütze*. He ran a gloved hand through his thick grey hair, surprised to find it stiffer, more bristly than earlier this morning. He replaced the peaked cap before Werther could see it and silently cursed the General-oberst for foisting this little brat on him.

He had court-martialled men for less impertinence than Werther had thrown at him throughout their slow drive into the heart of the Breton peninsula. But he had to remain calm. This was a major from the Schutzstaffel, not the Wehrmacht, and he had only limited authority.

Hartmann's reassignment from the Eastern Front had ostensibly been a favour, a reward for his bravery and leadership, but it made him feel devalued. His wounds had healed; even his psychological ones were no hindrance to his abilities. "Advising" the major was more like babysitting.

Werther had been put in charge of a squad of *Einsatzgruppen*. They were being groomed for deployment in Poland. To enforce the *Arbeitseinsatz*—the Compulsory Work Service—to supply fresh labour for the Reich.

A sledgehammer to crack a walnut, Hartmann thought

sourly. He'd seen the mobile killing squads in action in Lithuania, and the memory of their actions still sickened him.

Reports of a nest of partisans operating out of the pig farming village of Sanglier had led to the despatch of the team to investigate. It should have been a simple job, so simple Werther had insisted his team go ahead without him.

Simplicity had vanished when radio silence greeted each demand for situation reports.

"Firstly, *Major,* you will note that there is no body. The blood was spilled recently, last night. It was not a gunshot wound, because the blood is confined to one area."

"An execution, then. Held down, stuck like a pig —the way those peasants slaughter *their* pigs."

Hartmann shook his head irritably. "Not the action of the *Maquisards.* They shoot their prisoners. And more importantly, who took the body? Do you see any human footprints?"

Werther's pouted lips parted, as if a great thought had struck him, then closed. Then opened again. He looked like a landed fish, mouth opening and closing in an attempt to survive in a new, hostile environment. Out of his depth, Hartmann thought.

"Exactly. One pair. The soldier's own. The rest of the tracks are..."

"Hoof prints!" Werther scowled. "So where does that lead us? Perhaps those peasants at the village will say the devil carried him away."

Hartmann permitted himself a faint smile. "Maybe you are correct, Major. Old beliefs die hard here."

Werther crouched down and stared hard at the tracks in the frozen snow. The closest tracks were angled in their direction, pointing towards the frozen blood.

They were also very deep. The ungulate prints closest to the iced stains sank at least twelve centimeters into the snow.

"Whatever it was, it was heavy," Werther muttered.

Hartmann nodded slowly. A chill brushed the nape of his shaven neck, a chill that had nothing to do with the freezing winter air.

Werther stood up, a little too quickly. He brushed the frozen snow of his ankles, frowning at the blood that stuck to his boot heel. A small dagger of iced crimson attempting to pierce the polished leather.

"The village, Oberstleutnant. That's where we'll get some answers." There was an unhealthy gleam in the youngster's eyes. Hartmann knew all too well how those questions would be asked.

Werther looked at his watch. The sunlight glinted on the gold bracelet and Hartmann's eyes narrowed. That was not standard army issue. Another spoil of war, he thought, wondering if it had come from one of Werther's interrogation subjects in Paris.

Werther glanced back at him, unfazed by the disapproving glare.

"Don't look at me like that, Oberstleutnant. The nearest village to the field of operation that the squad disappeared from? It is obvious there is a nest of partisans there."

"And if there isn't?" Hartmann said icily.

"Then we'll be told exactly where they are." The young major spoke with smug satisfaction, relishing at the bloodshed to come.

Hartmann took one last look at the empty field. *Perhaps those peasants at the village will say the devil carried him away.* Despite himself, he shivered.

Werther was in the staff car before him, anxious to get warm—or perhaps he shared the staff sergeant's unease with the brooding landscape and its intimations of death. The driver had been visibly relieved when Hartmann permitted him to stay behind the driver's wheel.

Hartmann winced at the effort to traverse the short distance to the waiting Mercedes. The wound in his thigh was less than a year old, and occasionally it flared up, sending fresh waves of agony down his wasted thigh, the bone feeling as though it had never healed from being shattered. A reminder of the closest encounter he had ever had with death.

Not from a human foe.

He kicked the snow from his boots on the running board, but the memory of Stalingrad was not so easily vanquished. He sank into the back seat with an audible sigh of relief. The pain was sharper today, perhaps brought on by the cold. Or by the memory of those tracks in the snow—identical to the ones he had seen in Russia when he had received the wound.

They travelled in silence, the only sound the purr of the engine and the crunch of snow and frozen earth beneath the wheels as the driver cautiously moved the Mercedes W150 back on to the main road, heading east.

Several stretches were treacherous, and Werther loudly cursed the driver's caution. Hartmann was silent, approving of the staff-sergeant's insistence on slow speed. The Mercedes was a superb piece of German engineering, but it could not charge through frozen snowdrifts and bounce over potholes in the manner of the *Einsatzgruppen*'s ADGZ personnel carrier. Hartmann took pleasure in Werther's impatience as the hours dragged past.

The sun sank slowly, became a glaring ball of scarlet that painted the rocky terrain and sparse fields of Brittany in waves of scarlet, almost as bright as that frozen blood they had inspected. They passed several megalithic monuments in the snowbound fields; ancient stone structures from a forgotten past.

This was old, old land, Hartmann reminded himself. A land that didn't consider itself a part of France. He had seen much of Brittany, mainly the harbours and dockyards which were now used to launch the U-boat attacks on the Allied shipping convoys. The people were a distinct breed, as contemptuous of France as they were of its invaders. Generaloberst Köhler had warned him as he stepped into the port of Brest to be careful.

These are not mere peasants, Hartmann. They are close to their land, but also to their old beliefs. And you know how dangerous such beliefs can be...

Hartmann had known then that there was another purpose to his reassignment. He saw it in the watery blue eyes of his superior, the only person who knew what had happened in Russia.

A strange warning to part with, he thought. Since when is the Reich scared of old religions? Perhaps my reassignment has—

He was shaken from his reverie by the sudden braking of the Mercedes. The vehicle slid, fishtailing wildly until it came to a halt, angled towards a stone relic from a more recent time. Werther hissed an admonishment, backhanding the driver with one of his gloves.

Hartmann noted that the driver's hands were

shaking as he pulled on the handbrake.

"Something wrong, *Stabsfeldwebel?*"

"That, sir." The staff-sergeant's voice had cracked. Hartmann and Werther followed his trembling finger.

In front of the wooden village sign was a stone sculpture that had been reduced to rubble. Once an elaborately carved crucifix protecting sculpted figures of what looked like Mary and the apostles, its remains were half buried in the snow, as desolate as the megalithic menhirs and dolmens the three men had passed earlier.

"Just a Calvary sculpture," Hartmann replied. "A *Calvaire,* a common feature of these Breton villages. What of it?"

"It's been destroyed, deliberately...*but not by our unit, sir!* And look at the sign..."

The village sign was also covered in snow, and Hartmann could barely make out the village name: SANGLIER. But there was no mistaking the hand-scrawled words underneath.

ETERNELMENT VICTORIEUSE. The blood with which they had been painted had frozen, but not before it had dribbled down the post and pooled at the base.

More blood. This time, spelling out a warning and a challenge. Eternally victorious—and whose blood had been used to paint that?

This is not the action of partisans. Even Werther must know that, he thought, glancing to the now silent major.

Werther now seemed nervous. He was silent, swallowing noisily, and surreptitiously wiping the sweat from his top lip.

Fear, young man. At last you know what it feels like. But it was a fear he himself shared and had experienced before. Not the fear in the ruins of Stalingrad, a gut-wrenching fight for survival in an apocalyptic wasteland. Not the fear of leading a troop of men through the woods of Yugoslavia, being picked off one by one by the sniper bullets of *Heckenschützen* partisans.

Something was waiting for them in that village. And now Hartmann knew why he had been assigned to assist Werther. He smiled thinly while the major stared nervously into the distance, into the small collection of tumbledown cottages that formed the village of Sanglier.

Köhler, you sly old bastard. You knew what was waiting for them, and yet you sent them here anyway!

It was reassuring to know that others in the Wehrmacht shared his own hatred for the SS and the dishonour they had brought upon the German army.

"Onward," Hartmann said firmly.

The staff-sergeant swallowed and nodded quickly, nervously. "As you wish, sir."

It was more of a hamlet than a true village. Most of the cottages were in a bad state of repair, the thatched roofs unable to cope with the heavy snow. Faint smoke drifted from a solitary crumbling chimney in the central cottage. Dirt-strewn windows glared at the soldiers as the Mercedes made its way down the potted road into the centre of Sanglier, where the ADGZ armoured carrier of Werther's troop of *Einsatz-gruppen* waited.

Hartmann found it hard to tell which was the most recent building, for none of them looked to have been constructed within the last two centuries. Sanglier had none of the rustic charm of Pont-Saint-Esprite, or the beauty of the fishing village Pont-Aven.

The Mercedes drew to a halt beside the central

cottage, its fluttering wood smoke marking it as the least-inhospitable building. The motionless ADGZ was a mere few yards in front; doubtless its driver had made this building his first—and last—stop.

Bare brick showed behind peeling flakes of ancient whitewash, but the windows were open and there were signs of movement within. With the engine switched off, Hartmann could hear low voices accompanying the signs of movement. But while Werther eagerly climbed out of the car, Hartmann remained in the back seat.

"Oberstleutnant Hartmann!"

Hartmann ignored the major's impatient and impertinent summons. His attention was fixed on the pigs.

Five of them, squatting in the mud and snow churned from the Mercedes' wheels, motionless. Staring intently at the three unwelcome visitors to the village of Sanglier.

Where had they come from? Hartmann felt an icy chill caress the nape of his neck, and his war wound sent a sudden flare of agony shooting up his spine. He grimaced, but the pain did nothing to relieve the unease with which these beasts filled him.

The eyes of the pigs were focused solely on the SS major. Staring with an intensity that was almost human.

These were not domestic pigs. They were larger, at least five feet long, and their bulky bodies tapered towards their hindquarters. Their flanks were covered by thick coats of black, bristly fur that gleamed unnaturally in the dying sunlight. He thought they were hunchbacked for a moment, or at least had hackles raised like a dog's, until he recognised the dorsal crests. There was a strange smell in the air. The farmyard aroma of manure was accompanied by a distinctive leathery, peppery smell.

Wild boars. Not a domesticated hybrid, but the real thing. Their eyes glistened like pools of tar, and Hartmann thought he saw tiny pinpricks of scarlet within the centres.

Before Russia, he would have told himself that was ridiculous, just the effect of the dying sun. Winter sunset would make the glossy red patches on their unnervingly sharp trotters and gleaming white tusks look like blood.

He forced himself out of the staff car, pausing on the running board to allow the pain to fade from his leg, before joining the other two men. He pointed to the five boars.

"We have a strange welcoming committee, gentlemen."

The SS major did not reply. He stared at the empty gun turret and blood splattered side door of the ADGZ in horror—and then cold, mounting fury.

"*Murdered!*" His breath misted in the air, a cold plume of steam that hung over the Death's Head on his peaked cap like a cloud of gunsmoke. He opened the flap on his holster and withdrew his Luger, his eyes blazing in the direction of the cottage. He advanced, stiff with rage.

The door leading into the building was ajar. Werther thrust it aside with the toe of his boot. It crashed into the stone wall with a crack like a gunshot, pieces of plaster falling to the ground.

The ears of the five pigs pricked at the sound, the sole reaction from the otherwise motionless creatures. Hartmann glanced over his shoulder at them before following the other two men inside. Something else wasn't right.

There was only one occupant within, holding court behind a crude bar. The furious SS major kicked his way through the rickety wooden chairs and solitary table towards the waiting innkeeper, the dining furniture falling to pieces under his assault and creating small clouds of sawdust that slowly settled upon the uneven stone floor.

Behind the unvarnished wooden counter the innkeeper stood, towering over the podgy Werther. He was two inches taller than Hartmann's six feet, his wild mane of black bristly hair brushing the crumbling plaster of the low ceiling as he cocked his head and smiled quizzically at his visitors. He kept his shirt-sleeved arms folded loosely over his barrel chest, a casual, arrogant gesture towards the men of the Reich.

Perhaps he's been expecting us, Hartmann thought. There was something oddly familiar about the man, although he'd never met him before.

But I've met his type.

The innkeeper's smile broadened when Werther levelled his Luger at him. His unshaven cheeks wobbled with laughter, and a thunderous roar of amusement broke the stillness of the inn.

"Bienvenue, messieurs. I would put your toy gun away if I were you, little major." His voice was deep and harsh. Hartmann saw Werther step back, slack-jawed with astonishment.

The landlord reached under the bar counter and retrieved four shot glasses. He lined them up and poured an apple-scented liquor into each one. Werther's Luger dropped to his side, his mouth still agape.

"Too cold for cider, *n'est–ce pas?* This will put some warmth in your breath—and fire in your bellies, little men. *Salut!"* The innkeeper lifted his glass, toasted the stunned Germans, and swallowed the drink in one effortless gulp.

"You think this is *funny,* peasant?" Werther had regained his arrogant composure. The Luger found its way towards the innkeeper's chest again. "You dare to insult—"

"I do what I wish in my domain." His smile vanished, replaced with a tight-lipped sneer. His eyes burned with hostility. "Consider yourselves fortunate that I offer hospitality, when all you deserve is death. Now, *drink!*"

"The only thing I will be drinking is your blood, *drecksau!* Where are my men?"

The landlord's smile crept back slowly through his wild beard, but the fire in his eyes remained, with no hint of amusement.

"You answered your own question, little major. My *drecksaus*—the 'dirty pigs'—have more of an idea. Why don't you ask them?"

Hartmann turned to the nearest window. It was even filthier on the inside. He removed a handkerchief and wiped the pane in a circular motion. The handkerchief came away black with stale woodsmoke and cigarette stains. He peered through the window: the five boars were in exactly the same position. Still watching.

Too cold for cider, n'est-ce pas? This will put some warmth in your breath...

Now Hartmann knew what else was wrong with these creatures. The air outside was colder with the dying of the day, and the men's breath had misted in the air. Yet no vapour emerged from the snouts of these creatures. Their flanks flexed outwards and then inwards, but more out of memory—or imitation of—

breathing, than the actual act of respiration itself.

Yes. Russia all over again. This is why I've been sent here. He turned from the window and stared at the landlord.

"Werther. Holster your sidearm, and head back to the car. *Now.*" His eyes never left the glistening black pools of the landlord's. He was certain that he saw tiny red pinpricks in those dark orbs.

Werther shook his head in disbelief while the landlord nodded in approval.

"A wise decision, Oberstleutnant. I see you have encountered our breed before, *oui?* I noticed your limp. I myself have inflicted injuries identical to yours. It slows the quarry down...prolongs the glorious moment when the hunter realises he is now the quarry, as one of your troopers discovered last night. He got quite far...yet unlike him, you survived. How?"

Hartmann didn't reply. He was aware of the staff-sergeant and Werther staring at him quizzically.

"Come with me, my little war pigs." The innkeeper stepped past the bewildered SS major and approached Hartmann. He seemed even taller than before, and Hartmann forced himself to remain calm.

The innkeeper's beard was coarser, more bristly now, and when he smiled two large incisors peered upwards from his lower jaw. He swept past Hartmann and through the door. Hartmann glanced at the staff-sergeant and the major and inclined his head towards the door. He went first.

The boars greeted them with a subtle shift in their demeanor: muscles tensed and ready for action. The eyes narrowed, and the red pinprick of a scarlet pupil glowed within each dead eyeball.

"The boars have a special place in this region." The

innkeeper walked towards the first boar and stroked its flank lovingly. Hartmann noted the innkeeper's breath, like that of the boars', didn't mist in the cold air.

"They have a noble history here. They kept the invaders away. The Legions of Rome never conquered this region...*and neither will yours.* Your killing squad met their match here, and their deserved end." He smiled mockingly at Werther. "They squealed as we took them, little major. Brave soldiers of the invincible Reich? *Pah!* They shrieked like little girls as my children tore them to pieces."

He unbuttoned his shirt and allowed the visitors to see the set of six embossed metallic lozenges nestled in the bristly pelt of his chest. The identity tags of the missing *Einsatzkommandos* were stained with dried blood.

The SS major regained his composure, his arrogance and his self-belief. He lifted the Luger, took aim at the boar the innkeeper was lovingly stroking, and fired.

The bullet passed right through the beast's forehead, between the eyes, and travelled the length of its body. Dark black fluid gushed from the wound, splattering the innkeeper with a treacly liquid that glistened like sump oil and stank of putrefying meat.

But the boar remained standing. It didn't even flinch as the bullet passed through its body. Its flanks continued to expand and contract like a set of bellows, its eyes narrowed and burning into the major's in challenge.

Werther swallowed noisily and fired again. Another headshot. Then to the four others, a bullet in each one, firing until the magazine was empty.

The innkeeper stood slowly, wiping the black fluid

from his face. He shook his head sadly when he saw Werther reloading his Luger.

"You are wasting your time and energy, little major. *Les sangliers eternelment victorieuse.* They have always been victorious, driving away our foes in times of war. They always will be victorious. They are eternal."

Werther looked up. *"What?"*

"The armies of Germany are not the only ones who understand the concept of *Kadavergehorsam.* For you it means absolute duty and blind obedience until death, like good little war pigs. For us, we take the more literal meaning."

"Carcass obedience," Hartmann said dryly. He was back in the fields by the Volga, emptying his Sten gun's magazine into the huge boar that advanced unstoppably, shaking out the slugs along with the sticky black ichor that passed for blood in its undead veins.

"Exactement. Carcass obedience. Absolute duty and obedience...up to and *beyond* death. Their duty is, like ours, to the Old Gods. In return, the reward to *les sangliers* is eternity. A real, physical eternity, not that promised by the feeble Christ child."

Hartmann thought back to the destroyed Calvary sculpture outside the village, and the terrified staff-sergeant's words. *It's been destroyed, deliberately...but not by our unit, sir!*

"Your soldiers learned the true meaning of *Kadavergehorsam* last night. As you will learn now." He stood back and whispered *"Prenez-les, mes enfants."*

With lightning speed, the five boars raced towards Werther. The SS major let out a shrill scream when the first set of tusks pierced his left thigh, rising to a howl of agony and despair which would have had the ghosts

of his victims from the torture chamber of 84 Avenue
Foch smiling in approval. The leading boar drove in
deeper, tearing through muscle and snapping the thigh
bone. A jet of blood from the femoral artery splashed
the boar's face, soaking the bristles and snout. Werther's blood splashed into its eyes and the creature
didn't even blink.

Hartmann backed away slowly, his hand auto-
matically reaching for the flap of his holster. A soldier's
instinct, even though he knew cold steel would be as
ineffective now as it was in Russia. The flesh wound
flared again, but this time there was no pain. Now
warmth rapidly flowed through his body. A familiar
warmth, one he welcomed and feared at the same time.

The first two boars tore into the major's fallen
body, snouts burrowed into the soft flabby flesh of his
stomach. Coils of slippery intestines were dragged
across the frozen mud like grim carnival streamers,
steaming in the winter air. The other three boars
moved on the staff-sergeant.

Hartmann ignored the screams; they barely
registered. He lifted his Luger from its holster, and
threw it behind him.

He watched, dispassionate, as the boars tore his
comrades to pieces. Nothing was wasted. Not one scrap
of torn flesh, not one shard of splintered bone. Each
stitch of fabric, each polished button of the uniforms
and greatcoats disappeared into the bellies of the
beasts.

Only blood remained. Blood that slowly froze with
night's approach.

He watched the bullet holes in the boars fade,
knitted together with invisible needles; healing, becoming whole again. The gift of the Old Gods worked its

dark magic.

A similar dark magic worked its way through him now, a gift from the beast that had saved him from the wild boar in Russia—at the expense of its own life.

The fire spread through his guts, his arms and his legs, travelling to the furthest extremities. He felt the tingling in his scalp and skin as black bristles burst through.

There was disbelief in the innkeeper's black, red-pupilled eyes. Then a wry smile, obscenely large now that the tusks had fully formed.

"Formidable! That is how you survived my Russian brethren, *n'est–ce pas?"*

"A gift from the beast that saved me," Hartmann said with difficulty. His jaw extended with a meaty crack and his new incisors burst through his black gums. His smile was a snarl, and it pleased Hartmann to see the innkeeper pause.

"It recognised a valiant warrior. Gave you his power...and that is why your superiors sent you here, *wolf of the steppes!"*

"Boar versus wolf." Hartmann's smile was no longer human. The five boars looked up from the remnants of their meal. Steam wafted from their faces, warmth given by the blood of Werther and the staff-sergeant, and now Hartmann saw fear in *their* undead eyes.

"Sanglier contre le loup," the porcine innkeeper agreed. His hoofs scraped the ground; his dorsal crest shredded the remains of his shirt. "The dark power is in your favour. But the odds are in mine."

"We shall see."

Moonlight painted the bloody, snowbound arena of Sanglier a chilling silver.

And the boar of Brittany and the wolf of the steppes went to war.

Mounia Lakehal Meribout

The Wish

-"ONLY THREE PAIRS OF SHOES sold today, just enough money to buy semolina." Zulikha leaned over their little table with a sigh, wishing she had been able to provide her sisters with a better meal.

"People still wear shoes though!" Leila said.

"They just don't wear ours," said Baya. She stared at the sad and worried faces of her older sisters.

"The village is quiet tonight," said Leila, changing the subject from their endless money woes.

"The French are busy with the war. They don't have much time to scary us with curfew and night rounds," Zulikha answered with a certain bitterness.

"They stole Father from us, I don't understand why we, we, Algerians, are forced to fight this war and yet, it's the French problem, not ours!" Baya said.

"There's no point in bringing up painful souvenirs. Father is gone. Even if he had refused to join their army, they would certainly have killed him," Zulikha said.

"If he was French, they would have spared him from going there. A widower with three girls!"

"Baya please, we need to wake up early in the morning. So stop ruminating on the past and let's have a good night's sleep." As the oldest sister, she often assumed a motherly role towards her sisters. She washed the dishes, and by the time she was finished, her younger sisters were already in bed.

Zulikha awoke during the night, as she often did from worry. Leila had also awoken, and spoke to her quietly. "It's been a year already, isn't it?"

"Yes, it was last spring."

When their father had gone away to fight, the girls found themselves alone. They had an old uncle living a few houses far from their home who visited them from time to time to inquire about their health, but he was too poor to offer any material aid. Their neighbours were close and watched out for one another, helping where they could when one of their own fell upon misfortune. Now they were orphans, without parents and without husbands.

But, still, they did not feel themselves completely unfortunate. They had their house, small but cosy, the furniture consisting of two small tables and four chairs. For beds, they rolled thick sleeping mats on the floor every night. The house also served their workshop, where they made fine leather shoes. Zulikha prepared the sheep skins, Leila cut the patterns, and Baya sewed the pieces together.

Unfortunately, during these difficult times, money from a sale was rare. With the war, even the French were suffering.

But, still, this day had been a fortunate one. They had had a dinner.

The next day, the girls woke and finished their work early, for they had been invited to a wedding. Baya and Leila could barely contain their excitement as they walked to the celebration.

"Well, we will eat *chakhchoukha* for sure!" said Leila.

"And cakes," said Baya. "I just I can't wait to see the cakes!"

Zulikha smiled. "Try to behave yourselves little sisters, maybe some old woman will notice you and ask to marry her son with..."

"I don't want to marry," Baya said. "I want us to stay together forever!"

Leila tsked. "Don't be silly sister, if I find a suitable husband, believe me, I will not say *No.*"

Zulikha smiled, happy to see her sisters having a holiday. They would eat, dance, and laugh. Though life was hard, they were not so poor that they could not afford to add to the joy of the house. When they got to the party, they greeted their neighbors and offered their present to the bride: a pair of white leather shoes, perfectly made.

When it came time to be seated for the dinner, Leila and Baya stayed with the younger girls, all laughing and talking loudly. Zulikha chose to sit with the old ladies, as she found their gossip entertaining. Her attention was drawn towards two ancient crones who were leaning towards each other in earnest conversation. Zulika leaned closer, but not so close that she would appear to be eavesdropping.

"*...she managed to get her daughter married in a*

blink of an eye!"

"How did she do that?"

"As far as I know, she went to see Aicha/Kadir."

"And who are they?"

"No, it is the same person, we know her as Aicha but...her contact is a male: Kadir"

"Contact?"

"A sort of djinn, I think."

"Oh, this is scary. And are you sure that it worked?"

"The girl was about thirty-nine years old, she was not pretty and she had no money. She got married to a rich young man of thirty-two years old, within two months!"

"So old! And that quickly! And how much did they pay for that?"

"I don't know exactly, someone told me that this Aicha/Kadir had a strange way to...to get paid. I think she, or they, take something particular from each customer. It is not necessarily money...no, no... We must not even think about it, my dear. Those things are forbidden and dangerous. No one knows the price it."

"You talk witchcraft!"

The old woman looked around, then continued in a low voice. *"A few years ago, I heard about a couple with five children. They had five children and they could not make a decent living. So one day, the woman went to Aicha and asked for help. Aicha promised her wealth."*

"Did the family become rich after that?"

"Yes they did, but..."

"But what?"

The youngest child of the family lost the ability to walk a few weeks after the...visit."

"Was it an accident? An illness?"

"No accident happened and doctors did not detect any illness."

"You mean that..."

The hall filled with ululation. The old crones leaned closer to one another to continue their conversation, but Zulikha could not hear. She kept her eyes on their lips, straining to catch their words. The hall did not silence again until the dessert plates came around.

"...but most people are desperate when they go see them. They do not think much about the consequences."

Could that be true? Zulika considered. She wished she could have heard what price was paid, but knew better than to ask, lest she be thought of badly.

The wedding dinner ended with another chorus of ululation, and the women, both young and old, expressed themselves with local dances. Hair floated, hunkers shook, bare feet stamped joyously on the thin carpets which covered the dance floor. Men were not allowed here. Fathers, brothers and husbands made merry in a different hall, with their own excellent dinner and casual conversations.

Zulikha could not sleep that night. She kept thinking about this sorcerer, Aicha/Kadir. The story reminded her of another one that her mother used to tell her about a woman named Fatiha who wanted to marry a certain man. She went to a sorcerer and asked them to help her to marry the man. Everyone was astonished when after only a few weeks, the wedding was celebrated. It seemed odd that the nice young gentleman would marry that scold, for such was her reputation.

It did not take much time for this young man's mother to seek out the sorcerer, for she was convinced that her new daughter-in-law was a demon. She begged them to undo the enchantment and the marriage with it. The sorcerer proposed to cancel the bewitchment under a certain condition, that Fatiha must know about her mother-in-law's intervention. This she accepted.

As the sorcerer started their work, the woman returned home and went to daughter-in law. There she cursed both Fatiha and her son, saying: "You will never ever see my son again! This one has done this!"

The next day, her son told her he was going to travel to France. He kissed her good-bye, and indeed, she never saw him again.

Zulikha had always been frightened by the story. As she grew older, she thought her mother had just told her the story just to keep her from bad acquaintances. But now, after what she overheard at the wedding party, Zulikha was not so sure.

The next morning, after she had stretched the leather for the day's shoes, Zulikha left her sisters to go to the market to buy semolina, so she could cook galette for their dinner.

She came to the paved roads which told her she was coming to the town center. Up ahead, Zulikha saw a commotion. A crowd was forming, and the policemen were coming from all directions with their whistles. A man in native dress was shouting at a middle-aged Frenchman who wore a linen suit and a big moustache. Zulikha quickly understood that the Frenchman was the director of the local school, and that he had just expelled the first man's son.

"He is too old," said director.

"No, he has the right to continue, he's brilliant..." shouted the first man.

"You indigenes have got no rights. Go home and teach your child how to make tables and chairs."

"You will go to hell for this, I assure you! You are not worth more than a Nazi anyway!"

A stone-faced French police officer broke through the crowd and arrested the man. The director laughed. "You are already in hell! So keep it for yourself."

Zulikha felt sorry for the man. She and her sisters had been removed from school too. Her director had also cited the age matter. Always the same old excuse.

I wish I had finished my studies. She waited for the crowd to disperse while her dreams of what she could have been took her far away.

At market, Zulikha bought semolina and butter. As she was paying, she overheard two men talking about a new shoe shop that was about to open in her village. When she heard the address, her head spun. It was just in front of her house! Anguished, she was sure that this would mean the end for her and her sisters.

Zulikha dropped the bad news about the new shop on Baya when she got home. Baya cried so much that Zulikha couldn't help but drop some tears too. They decided not to work for the rest of that day.

"Who cares anyway?" said Baya. "Here comes Leila, now you must tell her too."

Leila came into the house, breathing loudly as if she had been crying.

"What happened to you?" asked Zulikha.

"He...he's leaving..." Leila could not continue.

"Who is leaving?" asked Baya.

"He promised to marry me as soon as possible, and now he is about to leave!" cried Leila.

"Who promised you marriage? He fooled you, didn't he?" Zulikha asked severely.

"No," Leila said quickly, "he is a respectable and

kind person."

"Where did you meet him anyway? And why didn't you tell us?"

"I wasn't sure about his intentions. I met him at... In fact, he owns the little leather store and he always greets me with smiles and adorable compliments...one day he just told me he wanted to marry me..."

"So this is why you always insist to go to the shop by yourself! Anyway, what happened?"

"They will take him to fight the European war."

"Dear God!" Zulikha and Baya shouted at the same time.

With nothing left to do in the day, Zulikha made the semolina into *gallettes* for an early dinner, though it was barely enough for the three of them. They ate in quiet, bad news stacked upon bad news. When the dishes were done, Zulikah went to Leila.

"Why you didn't tell me about him?" she asked.

"Because you're older than me and I felt it like treason," said Leila.

"I would have been very happy for you."

Leila lay down on her sleeping mat and cried herself to sleep.

The next morning, the girls had only a little cup of milk to share for breakfast. Zulikha spoke abruptly. "We need to find a solution, I'm not going to let us starve."

"And how do you think we can do that?" Baya asked.

"We can go find Aicha."

"Who is Aicha?"

Zulikha told them about the story she heard two nights ago.

"You really want to ask the help of a witch? Are you going insane?" shouted Leila.

Baya's eyes went wide. "We will be doomed for eternity."

"I don't think so," said Zulikha. "If we pay the price during our living days, I don't think we will be punished...*later.*"

"You are really scaring me sister, I never heard you talking like that," said Leila.

"I kept thinking and thinking about our future since our parents died," said Zulikha. "We don't have much of a choice."

"I don't agree. God gave us choice, we just have to be patient and work hard so..."

"So what, Leila?" Zulikha shouted at her sister. "We can't continue like this, we can't even afford to call a doctor!"

"But...sorcery...It is foolish! Do you remember the story mum used to tell us about the woman and her daughter in law?"

"Of course I do, but this is not the same case. We will not ask for making-up a relationship or breaking-up one. We will just ask for some fortune."

"But the price?"

Zulikha stood, her mind firm. "We will ask her and we will decide later."

Baya looked at their empty cup. "I have a bad feeling about that."

"Do you know how to contact this...sorcerer?" asked Leila.

"I found where the old Aziza lives. She gave me coffee and told me about where to find Aicha/Kadir, and said that they are very crafty and they can solve your problem in a blink of an eye."

"I guess we there's nothing to lose..." started Leila.

"Nothing to lose? And what about your soul?" shouted Baya.

"And how are we going to keep our souls in our bodies when that new shop takes away all of our customers?" Zulikha stared down at her sisters. "It will open soon. We will starve."

Leila knew she was stuck between two fires. She sighed. "I meant, we will lose nothing by just asking her. If the deal is unbearable, we will pass on it," said Leila.

Baya shook her head. "This is forbidden! You are playing with your soul, and I don't want to go to hell. Let's be patient and we will eventually find a solution."

Zulikha pounded the table. "Did you forget your sister's fiancé, Baya? We have to act quickly."

Leila burst into tears at the mention of her fiancé. Baya tried to comfort her. "We know that you feel responsible for us after our parents died but there must be another solution than selling our souls to a djinn," Baya said.

Leila dried her eyes and looked up at Zulikha. "Are you sure you want to try this, sister?"

"Yes. For all our sakes."

The three sisters remained silent for few minutes. Then Leila spoke: "We will go find this witch and then we will see."

The witch-house was about a half an hour's walk from their home, set high on a hill. When the sisters arrived at the front door, they were so frightened that they were actually shaking.

"It looks scary," murmured Baya.

"This is because of its reputation. The house is nice

yet," Leila said, trying to sound brave.

But Zulikha was determined to continue. She raised her hand and knocked.

An old woman opened the door. She stared at them for a few seconds then let them in without speaking a word. The hall of the house was large, so large that it made the sisters feel very tiny. The old woman showed a door at the end of the hall.

"It must be there...Let's go" Zulikha said.

"Are you sure, Zulikha?" Baya whispered.

"It's too late. We are doing it," Zulikha ordered. She grasped each of her sisters by the wrist and set off across the carpeted floor. Zulikha thought it took longer to walk the length of the hall than it should have, as if time itself refused to run. When they got to the door, it opened of its own accord.

The air inside the chamber was heavy with bakhour. The girls could barely make out a veiled silhouette within the clouds of scented vapor. Zulikha hesitated, then said, "Hello, we are here to seek..."

A woman's voice interrupted. "You are here to seek help I guess? No one comes to propose some."

The girls stood still, none daring to say a word.

Aicha continued. "What do you want exactly? Wealth, marriage, separation?"

Zulikha replied, "We want to secure our future."

"You want money or men?"

"We want enough money so we do not need to work anymore and...we want my sister's fiancé to stay in the country."

"Hum...You know there is a price, don't you?"

Zulikha answered. "Yes, we know about that, we also know that you do not take...lives, is that correct?"

Aicha laughed then said, "No, we don't."

Aicha put some herbs in a pot then lit a little fire and waited till the herbs burnt to ash.

Once done, Aicha spoke low with a man's voice. Zulikha felt Baya sag into a swoon beside her. She pulled up on Baya's wrist to keep her standing.

"Consider it done," said Kadir. "But there are some conditions: Go home and do not leave it until tomorrow. You may wake up at night and see some... *things*. So. Whatever you see, do not speak the name of God."

The girls looked at each other. "Why should we not speak of God?" said Leila.

Kadir spoke again. "Because this is magic. If you say something religious, it will undo my enchantment. It is just for one night. I believe in God myself. If you name him, my magic will disappear, but you will remain indebted to me. A deal is a deal."

Zulikha thanked him then asked if they could leave now.

Now Aicha spoke. "Before you go, I'm giving you an advice. The day you see a pink cat in your house, it will be the day you pay. Kadir is not in a hurry, so I suggest you avoid the sign. The later you pay, the better is for you."

The sisters turned and left the house much quicker than how they came into it. Baya was shaking, Leila was nervous, but Zulikha was becoming sceptical.

"A pink cat?" Zulikha shook her head. "Does such a thing even exist?"

Leila frowned, suddenly calmer. "A pink cat! This must be a joke!"

Baya refused to calm down. "It really wasn't looking like that sisters. They were awful!"

Leila adjusted her scarf over her hair. "Anyway,

what is done is done. It will happen tonight. I will make chamomile tea so we will sleep deeply. Then we will see."

Zulikha did not find sleep that night. She was very uncomfortable about the idea of banishing God's blessing *just for one night.* Just as she was about to drift off to sleep, she heard Leila scream.

Zulikha sat up suddenly. "What is going on with you, Leila?

"Shades!" Leila shouted.

Zulikha decided to leave her for the moment and check after her youngest sister. "I can't see anything, but I am hearing a sound, is that you Baya?"

Baya did not answer.

Zulikha groped around in the darkness for Baya until she found her huddled a corner.

"Talk to me Baya, please say something!" shouted Zulikha.

Baya was breathing loudly, but she did not say a word.

"Shades!" Leila shouted again.

Zulikha managed to assemble her sisters in her own bed, then tried to calm them without success. "In the name of Go..." Leila started, but Zulikha clapped a hand over her mouth.

"Remember what they told us! Just be brave." While she could not see Leila's shades, she could hear something eerie that the others did not seem to notice. *It's better they do not,* she thought, and pulled her sisters tighter, for the sounds were terrible. They clung to each other for the space of several hours, until the crowing of the cock announced the coming of dawn.

The unnatural voices ceased. Zulikha opened her

eyes, seeing the faces of her sisters looking back at her in the dim predawn light.

"They...the shades are not here anymore..." said Leila.

"And the murmurs are gone too..." Zulikha said. "We are safe now. Baya?"

"I...I wasn't able to speak" Baya explained.

"Did you...?"

"Yes, I saw the shades and I heard the noise..."

"You're in shock, we all are...Let's have some rest," Zulikha said.

They lay there, sleepless, until the light of day broke through the window.

There was nothing left for breakfast that morning. Just as Zulikha took Baya's hand to comfort her, she heard Leila shout.

"What again?"

Leila appeared at the door holding a box: "I found it on our table"

Zulikha took the box, then opened it while her sisters were staring over her shoulders.

The three girls shouted together. "Oh!"

In the box were a few gold coins.

"This is a fortune!" said Leila.

Zulikha shut the box. "The charm worked, we are saved!"

Leila and Baya danced with joy.

"Don't ever mention this to anyone," warned Zulikha, "and do not approach cats!"

But her sisters were too happy to even listen to her. They took their share from the box and went out to buy food and new clothes, and made a nice day of it, returning home quite late.

"Where were you?" Zulikha scolded. "Silly girls!

This is much too late to be out!"

"Oh Zulikha! Don't ruin the day!" said Leila.

Zulikha sighed at having to be the responsible one. "We were given a great present, nobody must know about that and don't forget that there is a price to pay, so be careful."

Her sisters ignored her, happily unpacking their purchases.

"What about...?" Zulikha asked.

Leila beamed. "He is supposed to enlist in a few weeks, so we can't tell if it worked for him yet, but... I'm quite confident he will not have to go!"

Zulikha smiled with her sister. *We did this to be secure and happy, so let them be happy,* she thought to herself.

From that day on, the little box produced gold pieces every morning, and the girls were able to live comfortably. They bought some furniture, clothes, a couch and even a small medical kit so they could skip having to find a doctor for certain emergencies. Life was easier, the girls were happier. Leila's fiancé enlisted, but he was not sent away. Soon they would be making plans for a wedding. Still, Zulikha anguished about the price to pay. She opened the book she was holding she and sat down to read.

Leila could not resist teasing her sister. "You barely know the alphabet!"

Zulikha did not look up. "I'm aware of that but laziness does not suit me."

Leila pushed the book away, making Zulikha look at her. "We are going out. Will you come with us?"

"And how is this different from laziness?"

Before Leila could answer her sister, Zulikha heard

heard a most terrifying sound, small and faint. The sound she dreaded the most since their day at the witch-house.

"Meow."

Baya entered the house holding a little cat. "Isn't he cute?" she said.

Zulikha was astonished. "Are you mad, or just an idiot?"

"What is wrong with you sister? It is only a cat!" said Baya.

"Don't you remember Aicha's sign?"

"But Aicha talked about a pink cat...This is a tiny white kitten," Leila said. She reached out to have a turn with the kitten.

"You are playing with fire," shouted Zulikha. "We should avoid all kinds of cats: Black, white, pink or purple!"

"I don't care. He is too cute. I am keeping it!" Baya said.

Zulikha did not sleep well that night. What an idea! Bringing a cat at home, those silly girls. She would have to get rid of it soon. They were living comfortably, and she was not going to let a stupid cat ruin that.

When Leila and Baya went out to go for a walk the next day, Zulikha stayed at home with the cat. She noticed a strange look in the cat's eyes, which did nothing to reassure her. She stared at the cat.

I am silly. All cats got that strange look.

The cat stared back at her, unblinking.

May it be the cat is announcing pay day?!

The cat flicked its tail back and forth, but its gaze remained unwavering.

I have to get rid of it!

Zulikha was too kind-hearted to harm the kitten, so she thought that if she scaried it up, it might go away. She took a brand from the kitchen fire and waved it at the cat's face, like she was going to scorch off its whiskers. The cat scampered backwards, but did not leave the house. Zulikha swung the flaming brand again; the flames danced backwards and burnt her hand.

"Go to hell!" she said to the cat, and went to get their first aid box to treat her hand. She found some bandages and a little bottle of mercurochrome with which to paint the wound. Just as she opened the bottle, the cat jumped at her face. Zulikha dropped the bottle and it fell, staining everything, including the cat.

When Leila and Baya got back home, they could not believe what they saw: Zulikha was crying loudly over a little pink kitten, quite dead in her hands.

"Oh my God!" shouted Baya.

"I tried to clean him up, but...I tried to wash him but he kept scratching me...So I..I...Oh my God, poor little thing!"

Zulikha was choking on her guilt.

"How did you manage to...?" started Baya.

"Drop it," Leila said.

Baya and Leila made some tea to help Zulikha to relax, but it had little effect.

"Come on girls, we have to stay calm," said Leila. She took the cat away to bury it.

That night, the girls had never been more scared in their lives. *Is this really pay day?!* They stayed up late, sitting up on their sleeping mats, frightened and expectant. As dawn began to break, they finally fell asleep, as nothing seemed willing to happen.

A few hours later, Zulikha awoke to Leila's screaming.

"Where are you? I can't find you! We fell asleep at dawn, why is it so dark?" shouted Zulikha.

She went to the table and to light a candle. She knew she had managed to do it, but...she still couldn't see anything.

Leila was still screaming, Zulikha tried to calm her down but her sister didn't seem to hear.

Baya sat in her bed, petrified. It was Baya who understood first, understood that this was pay day.

When Leila woke, she had tried to speak to her sister but she could not hear herself, she panicked and started to scream.

Zulikha had taken longer to wake, because every time she opened her eyes, darkness was still there. Leila's screams had awoken her, because she could not see the light.

Zulikha lost her sight, Leila her hearing, and Baya herself was now dumb. The ability to communicate with each other was gone for good. The girls were sure about that.

As sure as they were that there would always be coins in the box.

DJ Tyrer

The Castle at the Edge of the World

"TOLKIEN? Sounds German, you ask me." Findon sniffed, the sound echoing down the dark, stone stairway.

Thompson shrugged. "I don't know about that, but he has no love for the Nazis and a son doing his duty."

"I've read his book," said Smithson, "quintessentially English."

"The man knows what he's talking about," Thompson said as they reached the cavern at the bottom of the stairs. "He found the Book of Lost Tales on the Lonely Isle, beyond the Wall of Time and Space, and translated it. Nobody else knew about this chamber—"

"—but, I did," said the Professor, who was waiting for them in the cavern beneath Warwick Castle.

Thompson and the eight others joined the Professor and the priests who waited for them: One Catholic and one Anglican, both shifting a little uneasily.

The new arrivals wore vests of chainmail over their army uniforms and, over those, white surcoats marked with the red cross of St. George. On their heads, they wore the classic tin helmet of the British Tommy and each man had a sword strapped to one hip and a revolver on the other. Nine St. George shields awaited them, laid upon the floor of the chamber in a circle about a deep well at its centre.

The nine warriors took up position beside their shields and raised them up. They gazed down into the black depths of the well.

"Welcome," said the Professor.

The nine men acknowledged him. The Catholic priest moved to bless and anoint each of them in turn, while the Professor spoke.

"Nine Paladins to quest beyond the Wall of Time and Space and retrieve those sacred items that will save England in Her hour of need."

He looked them over and nodded with satisfaction.

"Three men of noble blood, three men of noble mind, and three men of noble heart: Nine Knights to risk the Wasteland and the dangers of the Castle at the Edge of the World. Do not waver and do what must be done."

He and the priests began to chant in Latin, a blessing upon their endeavour and a calling to the Way the men would take.

Each of them knew what was at stake, even if some still had their doubts as to its veracity: Somewhere beyond the world they knew—of it, but not in it—there lay a castle that held great power—power that could save England, or doom Her.

And, somewhere in Germany, in a chamber like this one, beneath a castle called Wewelsburg, nine dark

Grail Knights of the SS prepared to set out upon the same quest. Should they succeed...

There was a rumbling sound and the well seemed to widen and deepen, yet without perceptible movement, stone steps appearing from its walls, leading out of sight. The men gasped to see it, even Thompson, who had wholeheartedly believed in the truth of the tale Tolkien had told to them from the beginning.

Some crossed themselves, others clutched their shields tighter.

"There lies your path. God be with you and guide you."

Taking a deep breath, Thompson led the way, the others following after him, down into the darkness below.

"You can...taste the energy in the air." Smithson cast nervous glances about the well's shaft.

"Stout heart," said Thompson. "Stout heart."

The journey felt as if it were taking forever, an endless trek down the stairs, leaving the chamber far behind.

Thompson halted and raised his hand, then pointed. "There."

The shaft of the well had come to an end, the stairs descending through air to a bleak moor below. The scene was lit with a hellish red light.

"Be ready for anything."

It was impossible to tell if they were in a vast cavern with a roof above their heads or if the sky was that of another world and overlaid with impenetrable cloud. The source of the ruddy light was somewhere above them, but impossible to discern.

Ahead of them, far in the distance, rose a turreted castle.

"It is the Pit..." murmured one of the men, crossing himself.

"Stout heart."

Cautiously, they advanced across the moor in the direction of the castle.

"To the tower, Childe Rowland," muttered Smithson.

"Cheery." Findon's soft laugh was hollow.

"Remind me, was Rowland successful in his quest?" asked Thompson.

Smithson shrugged. "I forget."

"I hope we are," said Findon.

There was a rumbling, a vibration that rose from the ground through their feet to shake their entire bodies.

The men glanced at one another and drew their pistols.

Earth erupted, spewing over them, rattling against their helmets and shields.

There was an unearthly roar and a serpentine creature, armoured with thick, charcoal-grey scales, rose above them. It had no eyes, but a wide mouth from which smoke and sparks escaped. Two short, but heavily-clawed limbs twitched, scattering earth.

Despite its lack of eyes, the vast wyrm inclined its head downwards, as if observing them.

"Scatter!" cried Thompson.

They did so just in time, for a wave of flame spat from its jaws to wash over the earth.

The men opened fire at it, but their bullets pinged off its heavy scales without any hint of harming it.

"It's a dragon!" Thompson drew his sword. "We need to kill it as St. George killed his dragon."

It spat fire, again, and they scattered further.

Then, it lunged earthward, jaws snapping, and Thompson took his chance.

With a wild leap, he threw himself onto the back of the wyrm and seized ahold of one of its scales and held on for dear life as the beast bucked, trying to throw him off.

The others ran forward, braving the snapping jaws and slashing claws, to stab and slash at it.

"For God, England, and St. George," shouted Thompson as he swung himself down aside of its head and thrust his sword up into its mouth and into its brain.

The wyrm thrashed and shuddered, then fell to the earth and lay still, throwing Thompson clear.

He rolled into a crouch and stood, retrieved his sword.

A cheer went up.

Shaking his head, Thompson said, "We have a long way to go still, men."

They proceeded on their way, a long and weary journey across the seemingly-boundless wastes.

Findon halted and pointed skywards.

"What's that?"

Something dark and winged, like a bat, only with a long neck, with a lizard-like head atop it, and a viciously-barbed tail trailing behind.

"Another dragon, a winged one," somebody said.

"A griffin?" suggested Findon, drawing his sword.

"No." Thompson shook his head. "It's a wyvern: Two legs and wings—that's a wyvern, alright."

"But, can we kill it?"

Thompson looked at Findon. "We killed the wyrm..."

The beast swooped towards them and they opened fire, bullets tearing at the leathery wings, but not deterring it.

It flew over them, tail lashing, forcing them to dodge, then turned back and swooped in low.

Then Findon leapt aside as it soared towards him, slashed at it with his sword, opening up its side. He only just managed to duck beneath the sweep of its tail, its barb tearing his surcoat and sparking off his mail.

He cursed at the close call.

The wyvern shrieked and shot upwards, then veered back towards them.

Unwavering, Thompson raised his revolver and pointed it at it, carefully aimed it between the creature's eyes, fired...

It lost control and smashed into the ground in a tangle of limbs, twitched, then lay still.

Thompson looked at his gun in relief.

"Well, they *do* work down here..."

"Thank goodness," said Smithson.

Thompson laughed. "Two horrors, two successes, no casualties...we might just do this thing."

The rest of the journey passed without further incident, although they continued to glance about nervously at any potential threat, the slightest sound or shadow.

The castle, now, lay before them, tall and dark.

Two large figures in iron plate stood, one to either side of the open gates, one leaning upon a heavy mace, the other upon a battleaxe.

"Trolls, I'm guessing," said Smithson.

Findon shook his head. "Whatever they are. I don't much fancy fighting them..."

"Maybe we can sneak past?"

"We can try," said Thompson.

There was a sound of metal grinding against

metal: A troll had looked up at them.

"Ah," said Smithson, "I think they're spotted us..."

"So much for sneaking," said Findon.

Thompson shrugged. "They're smaller than a dragon..."

"True..."

Swords in hand, they charged at them.

Grunting in surprise, the trolls raised their weapons, holding them ready.

One swung its axe at Thompson, who managed to parry the heavy blade from cleaving through him, but was propelled backwards by the force of the blow.

The other swept four men aside with a single swing of its mace, shattering ribs and leaving them winded upon the ground.

Findon rolled beneath an axe-blow and thrust upwards, beneath its armour.

The troll howled in pain and fell to its knees, forcing him to scrabble away from its bulk.

Thompson had regained his feet and leapt forward and lopped off its head.

The second troll roared in anger and swung at him, but he dodged aside. Others distracted it.

Findon slashed at its leg, forcing it down onto one knee. Thompson dodged forward and finished it off.

Groaning and standing, Smithson rubbed at his ribs.

"That was less easy than I expected," he said.

Thompson shrugged. "Let's see what awaits us, inside..."

Had the Professor been with them, he would have been able to name the beings that infested the castle, but none of them knew quite what to call the long-limbed, fierce-faced, tusked man-things with skin like bloating corpses. Goblin seemed too mean, ogre too human, and ghoul too mindless for the mailed warriors they faced, who carried barbed swords and spears.

Using their shields to parry away the attacks, they fought their way through the heaving mass of in-human warriors, bullets and sword-blows cutting down those which stood before them.

"The central tower," cried Thompson, pointing with his sword. "That's where we'll find what we're seeking."

They fought their way on, but soon the mass of enemies thinned and they began to find corpses laying before them.

"Someone has already been this way," said Smithson.

"Damn Nazis." Findon spat.

"They must have come in through another gate. They can't be too far ahead. Hurry."

They began to run, cutting down the odd warrior creature that popped out to confront them.

"It's like a bleeding training exercise," shouted Findon.

"What the hell kind of training exercises did you go on?" Smithson retorted, shooting another of the castle's bestial guardians.

Thompson paused and leant upon his sword over the gutted body of one of the creatures.

"We *are* doing the right thing, aren't we? I mean, if these things are only doing their duty in guarding this place, doesn't that make us murderers and thieves?"

Smithson shrugged. "All we can know for certain is that those SS villains are ahead of us *and* if they get their hands on the power of this place..."

Nodding, Thompson began to walk again.

"Whatever our sins may be, the sin of failure would be a far greater one, indeed."

They hurried up the stairs towards the sounds of

battle atop the tower. There, in the highest chamber, they found the black-robed Knights of Wewelsburg with hooked crosses emblazoned in white upon their tabards and gilded upon helms, who had just slaughtered the last guardians of the castle. The white-robed body of a penitent or priest lay bloodied at their feet, cut by many more sword-blows than an unarmed, unarmoured man warranted.

The dark Grail Knights turned to observe the Paladins of St. George with featureless visors.

Thompson looked past them. Set upon a table covered with a cloth of the purest white were the three items the Professor had sent them to save from darkness: A golden sword, a silver chalice, and a shield decorated with a distinctive star. The Sword of David, the Cup of Christ, called the Grail, and the Shield of Solomon.

Beyond were wide unglazed windows that looked out upon an endless void that seemed to encroach upon the world as if it wished to devour it: This was, he knew, the Edge of the World at which the castle stood guard

Somehow, he wasn't sure how, Thompson knew that the void was what the Nazis served, or was the product of their evil, a nihilistic wave of destruction that threatened to engulf not just Europe, but England and the entire world. An all-devouring Nothingness that would take the castle if they failed and, in consequence, all they held dear in the world they knew.

"Kill them!" he cried and charged, sword in hand.

The battle was brief but brutal, a vicious melee of thrusting and slashing, parrying shields, and counter-blows, neither side offering quarter.

Three of the black-clad Knights of Wewelsburg fell

to the blades of the Paladins, but soon, only Thompson, Smithson and Findon remained to oppose them, each grievously wounded by stabs or slashes.

Disarmed, they were herded to one side of the tower room by five of the knights.

The sixth one surveyed them, his contempt palpable despite the visor of black iron that hid his face.

"So, these are the best England can muster? Just as our ever-glorious Luftwaffe command the skies, so do we command this place upon the cusp on *Ginnungagap*."

His laugh was a hollow echo.

Thompson spat. "Your evil will not stand."

One of the Knights kicked him and he doubled up with a groan.

The dark Grail Knight approached the table and called two of his fellows over to him.

In unison, the three black-clad Knights reached out to seize the three treasures of the Castle at the Edge of the World.

As their gauntleted hands grasped them, golden flames leapt from cup, sword and shield to run up their arms and engulf them.

Horrible screams escaped their helmets as they burnt.

The three Knights guarding the Paladins turned in shock and the flames leapt to them, burning them up in turn.

Within moments, nothing was left of the dark Knights, but ash which drifted slowly across the floor of the room to scatter out upon the breeze through the windows and fall into the void and oblivion.

"What the hell just happened?" gasped Findon.

Thompson laughed, unable to help himself.

"The fools fell victim to their own vile ideology! Ha! They called themselves 'Grail Knights' but were blind to the truth. They failed to grasp that the relics they sought to seize were the property of the Jews, the regalia of the royal house of Judah. No Jew-hater like them could expect to wield their power unscathed..."

He laughed again. "They were burnt up by their own unreasoning hatred."

Groaning in pain, he stood.

"Come on, it's our turn."

Findon hesitated. "I'm not sure I'm a Jew-friend... I mean, I've got nothing against them, but I've never actually met one...and, well, I'm scared..."

"You have no choice—it has to be done." Thompson shrugged. "It's time to find out if you're worthy. Still, you cannot be as unworthy as those Nazi scum..."

"True...Oh, here goes!"

The three men stepped forward and picked up the objects, which glowed, but did not burst into flame.

"The sword that smites," said Thompson, "the shield that wards, and the cup that heals. With these returned to England, the Wasteland shall be healed and, surely, victory will be ours."

Smithson nodded. "It's likely to be a hard slog, but I cannot see the Führer emerging victorious now. Let's get these home."

"But, don't let your guard slip, not till we're back in that cave beneath Warwick Castle."

"God save the King," said Findon, "and, we three, too!"

They descended the stairs, certain that victory was, now, within England's grasp, that right would prevail over evil once more.

Sean Patrick Hazlett

Serpent's Wall

-PAPA STORMED INTO THE COTTAGE, tearing off his sheepskin *ushanka* in a huff. "The chickens are missing!"

Yulia's stomach groaned—an instinct she'd honed during the famine. "We'll find them. They can't have wandered far," she said, knowing full well Papa would've already considered that possibility.

He shook his head solemnly. "No. The coop was torn open and covered in blood. Wolves, I suspect, though I don't quite know what to make of the scorch marks."

"Scorch marks?" Some dim childhood memory reminded her that that detail was important. A warning from Mama when Yulia was small. Something about fires above, fires below, and fires within. Dismissing the recollection as a distraction, Yulia concerned herself with more practical matters like how she'd replace the kolkhoz's missing livestock or how she'd explain their disappearance to the Bolsheviks. But before Yulia had a chance to formulate a plan, she heard a diesel engine rumbling outside. She shuddered. Ever since December 1943, when the Red Army had driven the Germans out of Denisi, the Bolsheviks regularly patrolled the area. To the West, the Red Army had pushed all the way to the outskirts of Berlin, where the Third Reich was desperately fighting for its survival. But the Nazis no longer concerned Yulia—the Bolsheviks did.

Papa nodded toward her cleavage. "Cover yourself."

Yulia blushed before donning a shawl. She'd been an awkward little girl during the German occupation. But now, at thirteen, Yulia was blossoming into a beautiful young woman at the most inopportune of times. She'd also begun to sense the unspoken whenever she was around others. Some villagers said Mama had been able to catch thoughts too, but Yulia'd never put much stock in those tales.

Papa opened the door to their state-owned cottage. Across a muddy field, a squat, slate-gray T-34 tank belched smoke like an old pipe. Three Bolshie soldiers climbed off a red star-stamped cupola and approached her and Papa.

Papa clutched her arm, trying to drag her back inside. She resisted. Like Mama had been, Yulia was fearless. The Bolsheviks, like the Germans before them, didn't scare her one bit.

Their leader was a bear of a man. Brandishing his rifle, he made it clear that Papa would be inviting him inside.

But Yulia could sense something else. She couldn't quite describe the feeling. It was as if she could smell his thoughts on the chill wind, thoughts that seemed eager for violence.

Papa and Yulia stepped aside to make way for the soldiers. As they crossed the threshold, the bear's lanky companions leered at Yulia.

Once inside, their leader said, "I'm Sergeant Gordunov and I'm searching for my comrade. His name's Anatoly." He held up a black and white photo of a boy with strong cheekbones and a wide smile.

Papa stared at the photo as if to make a point of taking the inquiry very seriously. He shook his head. "Can't say I've seen him. Perhaps he decided to take some leave?"

Gordunov scowled. "Anatoly's a loyal soldier. He's no deserter."

Papa held up his hands, palms facing outward. "I meant no disrespect. Just trying to be helpful."

"I bet the Nazis found you very helpful too," Gordunov said with venom. "You hear anything about his whereabouts, report it to me immediately." He pointed outside. "You can find me at our camp about a kilometer beyond that ridge." Gordunov turned toward Yulia and rubbed his belly. "I'm hungry. How 'bout a snack?" He grinned, revealing a mouth of missing and rotten teeth.

"Please," Papa pleaded, "the Germans cleaned us out. We've only just begun rebuilding the kolkhoz's stores."

"See," Gordunov nudged his comrade, "these Ukrainians were very helpful to the Nazis." Then he gripped his rifle and glared at Papa. "I'm sure you'll be even happier to help us, no?" The towering Russian wound like a cobra poised to strike.

Papa lowered his head and meekly motioned toward the kitchen. The soldiers tramped through the cottage, leaving clumps of mud in their wake.

Yulia stewed as the men rummaged through what little food they'd been able to save after fulfilling their state-mandated quota. Pots and pans clanged, and cupboard doors slammed open and shut.

Ten minutes later, the soldiers returned, carrying the family's last two loaves of bread.

Papa placed his hand on Gordunov's arm. "Please," he whispered, "leave something for us. We'll starve."

Gordunov sneered. "Like the rest of the Motherland, you'll make do."

The men left with their loot, reclining on the back of their T-34 as it rumbled southwest toward the bank of the Dnieper.

* * *

Yulia began tilling the field just before dawn. Her stomach grumbled. Later that night, her and Papa would dig up the bread they'd buried near the privy for emergencies like this.

With a drill plow harnessed to Olga, the kolkhoz's last surviving horse, Yulia churned the loamy earth into narrow ribbons and sowed the grain that would sustain them through the next winter. It hadn't always been this hard. Papa had owned several of his own horses before the Bolsheviks had confiscated them when Yulia was a toddler, during Stalin's collectivization campaign.

When the red-orange sun crested the horizon, a winged shadow drifted from east to west across the field. Casting her eyes skyward, Yulia watched the pair of black wings glide lazily on a chill wind. She followed them to a lonely oak perched on a hill. There, a committee of vultures congregated.

Yulia pulled Olga's reins taut. The horse came to a stop. She dropped the reins, patted Olga on the nose, and then headed toward the tree.

At the hill's summit, she found the wake of vultures gorging on a corpse. The bald scavengers were so engrossed in their feeding, they ignored her approach. As she drew closer, she recognized the partially eaten face of the boy in the photo, Anatoly. His eyeless pits stared into the void.

Fearless, Yulia drew closer still. She gagged on the stench of decay, then held her breath. Upon more careful scrutiny, Anatoly's torso appeared to be charred and blackened, reminding Yulia of Mama's eerie warning all those years ago.

Gunshots!

Two vultures exploded in a hail of feathers. The others took to the air.

"You there!" a man shouted in Russian. "Don't move."

Yulia's heartbeat quickened. From the valley below, Gordunov and his two lackeys stomped toward her. The sergeant put his paw-like hand on her arm. "You and your papa will pay for this."

"Please!" she begged. "I had nothing to do with this. I just found the body."

"Shut up, you filthy little *suka*."

Gordunov's backhanded blow to her face nearly knocked her off her feet. She could taste the salty tang of her own blood.

She struggled to keep up with Gordunov's long strides as he dragged her back to the cottage. Her arm throbbed from his grip.

When she and the Russians were within a hundred meters of the cottage, she spotted Papa. He stood outside, transfixed by the spectacle unfolding before him. Gordunov hastened his pace, hauling Yulia through the muddy field.

The sergeant smirked when he saw Olga. Olga responded with a warning snort. Her ears went stiff and started twitching. Gordunov shoved Yulia into the mud. He unslung his rifle and shot the horse from his hip. Olga collapsed with an ear-splitting squeal.

Yulia scrambled to her knees and crawled through the muck toward her dying horse. Tears rolled down her muddy cheeks, obscuring her vision. She placed her hand on Olga's flank and sobbed.

"That's what you get, *suka!*" Gordunov roared.

Papa raced to Yulia. One of Gordunov's henchmen swept Papa's legs. Papa careened into the mud. When he tried to stand, Gordunov's henchmen battered him with their rifle butts.

Gordunov held up his hand. His cronies stopped pounding on Papa. "Who tortured and killed Anatoly?"

Papa's eyes widened. "I...I don't understand."

Gordunov kicked Papa in the face. A riot of teeth and blood sprayed from his mouth.

The two men resumed Papa's beating. Their anger now seemed completely unhinged. She could smell thoughts reveling in the bloodlust. And she knew for certain that if she didn't intervene, they'd kill Papa.

"Stop!" she yelled. The soldiers laughed while they pummeled her father.

She crawled back to Gordunov. The sergeant observed the savagery as if he were appreciating Russian folk dancing.

"Please," she pleaded. "Let my father go. If you kill him, you'll have to answer to your commander. And since the horse you shot was also state property, you might have to answer for that as well."

Gordunov's rotten grin evaporated. He looked down at Yulia with an expression of contempt. Folding his arms across his chest, he paused, then said, "Blokhin. Kablukov. Enough!"

The two men obeyed, backing away from Papa, who now lay quivering in a pool of blood.

Gordunov thrust his meaty index finger at Yulia. "You. You're too smart for your own good. If you don't supply names by tomorrow, we'll tell the Molokan your papa did it. Then we'll get a warrant to shoot him."

Yulia shivered. She'd only heard mention of the Molokan in hushed whispers among the villagers. It was widely rumored that he drank the milk of the soul. Yulia didn't put much faith in such stories, but she nodded with an enthusiasm that shamed her anyway. A bullet would kill Papa more surely than some superstition.

She clung to her broken father as the soldiers marched off.

*   *   *

Vivid images of smoldering fields and men engulfed in flames invaded Yulia's dreams. From the vantage point of some winged beast, she watched the world burn. The visions were so visceral, they roused her from her sleep. A sudden urgency burned inside her gut. She hastily got dressed and scrambled outside into the welcoming night.

Strangely, she felt drawn to Serpent's Wall, a series of ancient earthworks stretching across the Ukraine. A collection of oak, birch, walnut, and chestnut trees crowned the earthen mound, their leaves just beginning to sprout in the spring thaw. Built centuries ago by some long-forgotten people, the Wall exerted a magnetic pull on her.

As she trudged through the darkness like iron to a lodestone, something in the distance reflected the moon's silver light. As she walked further, she could make out an oval-shaped object nestled against the earthen mound. An egg as tall as she was rested against the wall.

She pressed her hand against the egg. It had the texture of a homemade clay pot, imperfections and all. The steady rhythm of a heart beat inside. Something deep within her mind's eye called out to her. Visions flooded her consciousness, overwhelming her senses. Images rife with scales, fire, and fangs buffeted her at such a furious pace she couldn't process them.

She yanked her hand from the egg. What did it all mean? What kind of creature could produce such a thing? Why was the being inside reaching out to her? While Yulia had more questions than answers, she knew deep within her bones that the egg was linked to Mama's secret: Mama's stubborn insistence that the family never stray far from Serpent's Wall, especially during the famine when leaving the farm could have saved Mama's life. No. Yulia had no doubt the egg was worth protecting. She just didn't know why. Unsure what to do, Yulia made her way back home, blundering south along the Wall.

"Who goes there?" a male voice said in Russian. A flashlight's bright rays washed out her night vision. The metallic click of a rifle echoed in the gloom.

"Yulia," she shouted, holding up her hands.

"Well, Yulia, a bit late to be wandering out in the dark, isn't it?"

She nodded.

Behind her, something rattled.

"What was that?" said the man. "Yuri, you and Dmitry go check it out."

"Yes, Lieutenant!" Yuri said. He and Dmitry bounded into the night. Three other Bolshies stayed with the Lieutenant.

Yuri shrieked.

"Everyone, down!" the Lieutenant commanded.

He delivered the order with such authority that even Yulia dove into the dirt.

The flashlight's ray danced chaotically and then stabilized. A black, sinuous thing briefly darted into the light, then back into the blackness.

"The hell was that?" said the Lieutenant, his voice quavering.

Dmitry squealed.

The Russians unloaded their weapons. Yulia closed her eyes and curled into a ball, making her body as small as possible. Hot shell casings rained down all around her. The odor of gunpowder suffused the cold night air. Yulia covered her ears in a futile attempt to mute the deafening gunfire.

In minutes, the shooting stopped. Slowly, Yulia opened her eyes. Just meters away, something slinked in the dark, tearing into the Lieutenant's bloodied leg. Six glowing ruby-red eyes regarded her from a moon-cast shadow. Then, as quickly as it appeared, the thing slithered off into the night, leaving six dead Russians in its wake.

*   *   *

Yulia woke in her bed to the sound of splintering wood. After returning home, she'd decided to wait until morning to tell Papa what she'd witnessed. Now, she feared she might be too late.

A loud crash shook the cottage. Yulia leapt up in a panic. She dressed frantically.

Footsteps tramped through the cottage and then up the stairs toward Papa's bedroom.

"Get up!" Gordunov's distinctive voice growled through the wall.

Yulia bolted out of her room and slammed into Blokhin. She fell backwards. He caught her. He spun her so her back faced him. He pulled her toward him, then cupped her breast. She stomped on his boot, broke free, then slapped him. She rushed past the soldier and into Papa's room.

Gordunov had Papa by the scruff of the neck and was dragging him toward the door.

Papa shouted. "What's the meaning of this? I've done nothing!"

"Then why do our comrades keep turning up dead or missing near this farm? You lie! Who are you protecting, old man?" Gordunov backhanded Papa in the face, peppering the chalky wall with blood.

Papa regarded her with his rheumy eyes. "Run!"

Gordunov's lackeys made to grab her, but she bobbed and weaved until she passed through the shattered front door and into the furrowed field. A thick orange sliver pierced the eastern horizon.

A storm of anxiety raged within Yulia. She worried for Papa's safety. She imagined the worst when it came to his treatment at the hands of the Bolsheviks. She was troubled that they were also coming for her. And she fretted over the egg. What if the Bolshies had found it?

Yulia ran harder, terrified that if the Soviets had uncovered the bodies, they might also have discovered the egg. She feared she'd never see it again.

When she reached Serpent's Wall, the corpses were gone, but a blood trail led north. She shivered. If they'd come first, the Russians would've have taken the bodies and the egg. She had no desire to follow the trail, but she needed to know if the egg was safe. So she crept north along the Wall.

To her relief, the egg stood where she'd last seen it, untouched. She'd be damned if she let the Bolsheviks take it, so she gathered whatever sticks and twigs she could and covered the egg. Then she coated her scaffold with mud before she collapsed against Serpent's Wall and drifted to sleep.

*   *   *

It was dark when Yulia woke. How she'd slept through an entire day was a mystery to her.

She sat up against the Wall. Six glowing eyes regarded her from the blackness. They crept closer. Moving tentatively at first, they soon advanced with a steady confidence that frightened her.

In half a heartbeat, three wedge-shaped reptilian heads craning from serpentine necks snaked toward her. Without its wings, the creature's scaly frame was as wide as a German shepherd. It was over three times as long, including its necks and barbed tail. As if by instinct, Yulia held out her hand. In turn, each head sniffed her tender palm. Then the necks slackened, and the beast sauntered forward like a puppy meeting a new friend. Childlike, it settled into Yulia's lap, nearly crushing her with its not inconsiderable weight.

Yulia couldn't help but smile. After all that had happened these past few days, she really needed this. The hatchling licked her with its three forked tongues, and despite herself, Yulia giggled. She hugged her new friend with as much love as she could give.

Then, with the swiftness and suddenness of a snake, the rightmost head whipped back and gazed into her eyes. An avalanche of images assaulted her mind's eye. Warriors on horseback fired arrows at armored men and women manning a great wall. Just as the riders were about to overrun the battlements, streams of molten fire doused them from above. Then Yulia briefly glimpsed a scaled leviathan in flight.

The images appeared to shift forward to a time closer to her own. A skeletal woman shambled through a muddy street, begging a Soviet soldier for food. Relatives Yulia recognized from old family photos collapsed while swarms of flies gathered in their masses to feast on the great human harvest. *Holomodor*—the butcher's bill for the greatest collectivist enterprise in history. A utopian vision painted on a canvas of human skin, stretched raw from inhuman suffering. Over and over, she witnessed her countrymen suffer famine's slow death. And over and over, she swore she'd make the Bolsheviks pay.

She came to in a cold sweat. The sun crested the eastern horizon. The hatchling was gone, but the hidden egg remained.

* * *

The stench of diesel fumes and motor oil hung over the farm like a gray cloud. Yulia crept into the cottage, careful not to make any noise. In the near silence, she heard labored breathing.

Papa!

She raced upstairs. In his room, Papa cowered beneath his sheets.

"Papa!" she cried. "Are you all right?"

When he emerged, his face was bloated like a turnip. With what seemed like great effort, he sat up. His deep cerulean eyes gleamed in stark relief against a crooked nose and bloated black and blue cheeks. His smile was a small triumph against a swollen jaw and rows of jagged and missing teeth.

"I'm happy you're safe," he mumbled through puffy lips. "They want to talk to you."

"No. I won't speak to anyone who would do this."

He raised his right hand in supplication. "Please. Do it. They just want to ask you a few questions about the night those men died. They think you know who did it."

Yulia clenched her jaw. "No. I won't help them."

Engines rumbled outside. Yulia pulled back a curtain to look down below. Nearly a dozen tanks rolled into the field, ruining the furrows she'd tilled and jeopardizing her livelihood.

Papa gripped her arm. "Promise me you'll help them. If they take you away, they'll do worse things to you than they ever did to me. Please."

Yulia watched the scene below, her jaw set in grim determination.

* * *

They called him the Molokan. Some say the colonel was a mystic from the Siberian wilderness. Others whispered he possessed knowledge that allowed him to reach through death's veil. True or not, there was something unsettling about the man on her doorstep, the one staring into her eyes. Seeking, probing, testing.

She glared right back, finding solace in her defiance.

The pride in which he wore the black patch over his left eye could have only been earned through the deprivation of war. When his battalion had first set up camp, locals gossiped that the Molokan had lost his eye fighting an SS platoon hand-to-hand behind German lines in Stalingrad. Darker versions of the tale suggested he'd survived by hunting and eating Germans in the night. Some even hinted he'd devoured their souls.

The staring contest continued for what seemed like an hour. Neither the Molokan nor Yulia would yield. But the longer Yulia suffered his watchful gaze, the more vulnerable she felt. It was as if he was reaching inside her mind and plucking out memories.

As she glowered at the Molokan, despite her best efforts, her mind wandered. Before she became conscious of her thoughts, Serpent's Wall materialized in her mind's eye. She thought about the hatchling and all the visions it had granted her.

The Molokan smiled.

She closed her eyes and turned her head to avert his gaze, shutting her mind to the intrusion. But it was too late. Yulia panted, terrified he'd learn where she'd stowed the egg. He grabbed her chin, swiveling it back toward him. A powerful compulsion to open her eyes gripped her.

She fought against the urge, but the Molokan's will was too strong. Yet her mind seethed with a quiet fury. Drawing from this reservoir, she lashed out at her interlocutor.

The Molokan lurched backward in apparent confusion, shaking his head and stumbling like he'd been walloped with a frying pan. His smile curled into a scowl.

Yulia backed away in disbelief. Perhaps the stories

about Mama had been true. After regaining his balance, the Molokan advanced into the cottage, his glare filled with malice. She tried to strike again, but her well was empty. A tidal wave of psychic force swept over her. Her vision faded to black.

* * *

Yulia woke in a muddy field. The Molokan poked her side with a stick. The sky was dark and gray, with a looming storm on the horizon. Groggily, she rose to her feet.

He prodded her forward as if taking a cow out to pasture. Her heart sank when she realized he was leading her to Serpent's Wall.

Along the path, she passed soldiers placing plywood planks across a hole as wide as a tank and nearly as deep. It reminded her of the pits the Germans would dig to hide their tanks. One side had a gently sloping ramp leading into the hole so the tanks could roll into and out of it with ease. The Bolsheviks covered the plywood with tarp and then concealed the tarp with dirt. Near the ramp, a squat T-34 sat, its engine idling.

Two men ushered her toward a solitary wooden post ten meters from where she'd last encountered the hatchling. They pushed her face against the stake and then bound her with thick hemp. The rope bristled against her skin.

"Ah, my filthy little *suka*," Gordunov taunted from behind, "I'm gonna make you pay for running away."

That she couldn't see Gordunov only heightened her terror. What were the Molokan's plans? Why was he using Gordunov as his instrument?

The sharp crack of a bullwhip reverberated through the air.

"You hear that, *suka?*" Gordunov said. "Get used to that sound. The next time you hear it, my whip will be tasting your flesh."

Yulia's eyes widened. She glanced at the men who'd bound her, seeking a sign of what might come. They chuckled. She looked over her left shoulder. Her eyes settled on the Molokan. He seemed to regard her plight with disinterest.

"Why?" she squealed, immediately shamed the instant the word escaped her mouth. No. She'd suffer with dignity. She was better than these animals and she'd prove it.

The first lash beat the breath from her lungs. The second tore into her flesh. On the third lash, she bit her tongue, and it took every bit of self-discipline not to cry out.

She tried to strike out at the soldiers with her mind. But the pain of the whipping had somehow clouded her focus.

When the whip struck her a fourth time, she whimpered. Her vision faltered, and she now saw the world through a grainy gray film. She couldn't take the agony much longer.

On the fifth lash, Yulia detected the hatchling's presence nearby. It must have sensed her pain through their psychic link. Moments later and in broad daylight, the hatchling surged from the tree line along Serpent's Wall. It raced at a half gallop, half glide as it attempted, but failed, to fly. A Bolshie approached it slowly, and the hatchling incinerated him in a jet of flame.

The scent of roasting meat wafted through the air, adding flavor to the salty tang of Yulia's own blood. Gordunov rushed past her, gesticulating with his bullwhip.

One of the hatchling's maws yanked off a man's arm and swallowed it whole. Another engulfed a fleeing Bolshevik in flames.

Undeterred, Gordunov established a line of soldiers facing the hatchling. They advanced, firing a steady volley of rounds. The creature's hide appeared to protect it from the brunt of the assault, but it snarled when a few bullets slipped between its scales. Soon the hail of fire became so intense that the hatchling retreated backwards toward the dirt-covered tarp.

To Yulia's dismay, a T-34 rotated its turret and fired a round at one of the heads, cleaving it off. She muffled a scream. The Bolshies jeered as they herded the hatchling toward the trap.

When it seemed the hatchling could no longer breathe fire, it gnashed with fang and talon. Through their psychic connection, Yulia warned the beast to steer clear of the hole, but it wouldn't listen. The volume of fire was so overwhelming that an instinctual avoidance of pain dictated its actions now.

Then something miraculous happened. In the smoldering embers of the creature's headless stump, something wet and bloody bubbled into life. In less than a minute, the hatchling had regenerated its lost head. With renewed vigor, it advanced against the Russians, ripping them apart with talon, tooth, and claw.

Yulia smiled and then turned her head to gloat at the Molokan. When she saw him, her grin faded. His calm and confident demeanor suggested he'd anticipated this.

Another tank round slammed into the hatchling in a gout of smoke, flame, and guts. The Soviets renewed their offensive and the creature stumbled backwards toward the hidden pit. A meter from the hole, the wounded hatchling fought an inspired rearguard effort, severing another soldier's arm with its talons.

With a hand signal, the Molokan ordered a wave of reinforcements to rush into the breach and drive the hatchling onto the covered hole. The sound of snapping wooden planks echoed against the surrounding tanks.

The Molokan motioned toward the tank commander standing in the idling T-34's turret. The commander, in turn, ordered his driver to roll the tank down the ramp and into the pit, smothering the hatchling under tons of steel.

The tank pitched, yawed, and rolled like a rowboat navigating through a Black Sea storm as the hatchling struggled to escape.

An avalanche of psychic pain overwhelmed Yulia. The hatchling screeched in her mind. She could feel the tank's weight crushing the creature, squeezing out its insides.

Then the agony faded as Yulia's psychic connection was severed. Her eyes cast daggers at the tank commander. Intense fury welled up inside her like a boiler set to burst. She directed her spite toward him and let loose.

His head exploded in a riot of bone, brains, and blood.

She watched in disbelief. Seconds later, someone grabbed her shoulder. She turned her head, coming face to face with the Molokan. One gaze of his steely eyes drained the color from her world. Then, oblivion.

* * *

Yulia woke bound to an icy steel table in a pale green and windowless room. A blinding white light swayed above her.

Cold and clinical, the Molokan said, "She's awake."

"Let me go!" she yelled.

"Now, now," the Molokan said in a mocking voice, "you know very well we can't let you roam free. You're a deliciously dangerous girl."

As her eyes adapted to the brightness, she spied a row of eight uniformed male and female Soviet officers sitting to her right, scribbling diligently on notepads. To their right and at the opposite end of the room, Papa was naked and tied to a chair.

Yulia struggled against her bonds, masking her fear with an indignant scowl. "Papa!" She faced the Molokan. "You let him go! He has nothing to do with this."

The Molokan nodded in that patronizing way of his. "Yes, yes. All in good time, my girl. If you play your cards right, not only will I release your father, but I'll make sure you flourish under the Soviet Union's tutelage."

For a moment, she ceased struggling. She couldn't quite believe what she'd heard. After all, she'd murdered a soldier in cold blood and in front of the Molokan's entire battalion. The NKVD murdered people for far less.

He smiled in that cold way killers do—a grin of the teeth, but with predatory eyes that never falter.

"Your abilities are...impressive," he said. "So impressive, in fact, that the Revolution needs them to fight fascism."

Either sensing her confusion or just filling the silence, the Molokan continued. "It would be a good, respectable life. The Soviet Psychic Service occupies a position of great respect and authority in Comrade

Stalin's eyes. We'll help you develop and hone your gifts."

Yulia slowly nodded at the offer—not to accept it, but to show she was considering it. But despite her best efforts, she couldn't hide her hatred for the Bolshies. She could never stomach working for a regime that had starved her people; soldiers who had beaten her father; and a butcher who had killed a baby hatchling. "Go to hell."

"Been there. It was not to my liking." The Molokan cracked his fingers. "I thought you'd refuse." He clapped his hands. "Vasily, Anastasiya!"

Two of the note takers snapped to attention and walked toward Papa. They gazed into his eyes. Papa shook. The veins in his forehead throbbed. He shut his eyes and screamed.

"Stop!" Yulia shouted.

The Molokan moved to within centimeters of her face. "I see I now have your attention. Good. I can make your father's pain go away. All you need to do is join us."

A tear rolled down Yulia's cheek. An uncontrollable rage roiled inside her. With every fiber in her being, she lashed out at the Molokan.

Nothing.

He smiled that demeaning smile that said he had everything under control; that he had the situation well in hand. He clapped again. Vasily and Anastasiya returned to their seats. The Molokan pointed his forefinger at Papa and the bone in Papa's upper arm snapped and popped out of his skin.

Yulia shut out Papa's wailing and focused her mind on her bonds, trying desperately to remove them.

The Molokan laughed. "Child, your ability to manipulate bioplasma is confined to telepathic—not tele-kinetic—pathways. You can convince a man to boil his own mind, but you cannot use your mind to manipulate physical objects."

"There's an egg!" a raven-haired woman said, jumping to her feet.

Yulia almost cried. This entire time, the officers had been trying to read her mind. Now they knew about the egg!

The Molokan grinned. "Excellent! It seems we might yield two successes today. Now back to the other matter." The Molokan waved his hand. Papa screamed as a bone on his right index finger pierced the skin. "I can do this all day." The Molokan waved his hand again. Another finger bone shattered. Then another and another.

"Kill me!" Papa screamed. "Please! Kill me!"

"Oh that won't be necessary," the Molokan said in his smug tone. "Your daughter will protect you." He faced Yulia. "Won't you, Yulia?"

She sobbed. If only she said, "yes", she could stop Papa's suffering. But to what end? To serve an evil and murderous regime no better than the Nazis?

Papa screamed again. "Kill me!"

In his horrific agony, Papa gave her the only way out.

So Yulia annihilated Papa's mind, destroying the only leverage the Molokan had over her. As Papa sank lifeless into his chair, she howled. In her despair, her mind wailed...and a distant inhuman voice answered.

*   *   *

Yulia sobbed in the back of an American Willys Jeep, seated beside the Molokan. The Jeep rode at the tail end of a convoy that included a column of T-34s, a mechanized crane, and a flatbed truck. Yulia wanted desperately to lash out at the Bolshies around her, but she felt the Molokan's psychic cronies shielding her mind.

As the convoy neared Serpent's Wall, Yulia's depression grew deeper and more desperate. She hungered for death—an end to the psychological torture. They'd stolen everything from her, and now they were going to take the hatchling's unborn sibling.

The tanks fanned out in a horseshoe facing the earthen wall. The Jeep came to an abrupt stop. With nothing left to lose, Yulia chomped on the Molokan's hand, then darted out of the Jeep toward the hidden egg.

There was a chorus of mechanical clicks. Dozens of peasant soldiers trained their rifles on her. But she didn't care. If death took her here, at least she'd find solace in her final act: protecting the unborn hatchling.

The crack of a rifle shot and the zip of a bullet jarred her from her run. Another shot, this one closer. But still she ran.

Seconds later, she reached the egg and embraced it, protecting it with her body.

"Cease fire!" the Molokan yelled. "We aim to take the object unscathed."

The soldiers lowered their rifles. Gordunov charged forward and pried her off the egg. He dragged her back to the Jeep as easily as he would a ragdoll. In a futile show of force, she scratched him.

"Poor little *suka* lost her friend," he said, grinning.

Yulia wept in anguish as the crane rolled forward, hoisted the egg from the earth, and set it on the flatbed truck.

She howled. Her mind flailed at everyone around her. But the eight psychics had her mostly contained. Mostly. They couldn't prevent her from feeling the unborn dragon yowling within the egg. Its helpless pleas made Yulia scream over and over again. She wanted to tear her eyes out.

Yulia glared at the Molokan. He smiled back. Somehow, he could also sense the unborn dragon's anguish.

The ground shuddered.

The Bolsheviks looked around nervously. It grew quiet again. But the silence had the same aura of unreality as the eye of a storm. The air was still, but charged. One match and it would all blow.

The earth groaned with the strain of something massive burrowing toward the surface. A shower of mud, rock, and dust exploded from the earth. A snout as long as a column of four tanks pierced the ground and shot upward as its sinuous neck reached for the sky like a beanstalk. Two more heads followed, blanketing everyone in soil and upending three T-34s.

Giant ribbed membranous wings ending in talons launched into the slate gray sky, casting a long shadow. It was the largest creature Yulia had ever seen. As the dust settled, the soldiers stood dumbfounded, watching the great winged beast soar toward the horizon.

Then it wheeled back around, picking up speed. The giant wyrm swooped down like an aircraft on a strafing run. Its three heads blazed a flaming path, combusting men and material. Survivors unloaded their automatic weapons pell-mell at the beast.

After it had completed its pass, the dragon clutched the egg in its colossal talons, disappearing over the horizon.

The soldiers scrambled around a chaotic scene, fighting fires and collecting the charcoaled remains of their dead.

Minutes later, a black speck appeared in the distant sky, quickly resolving into the three-headed wyrm. It no longer carried the egg. As it approached, the Bolshies threw together a hasty defense, aiming their rifles and rotating their tank turrets toward the flying leviathan.

The lingering scent of sulfur suffused the air as the dragon swooped down on the Russians. It blazed another swath of earth, metal, and men, fusing them into ash. Rifle rounds ricocheted off the beast like ball bearings bouncing off concrete. But sometimes a round would slip between its scales, causing it great pain that Yulia could sense through their psychic link.

Not only did the dragon have to contend with an all-out physical assault, but Yulia could also feel the Molokan and his psychics assailing the dragon's mind. It was if the dragon were playing multiple games of chess simultaneously.

While the psychics concentrated their efforts on fighting the dragon, shielding Yulia no longer seemed a priority. So Yulia surreptitiously took control of a soldier's mind, compelling him to creep behind his comrades and slit their throats. She killed three psychic officers in this manner before attracting the Molokan's attention.

A wall of wind swatted her from the Jeep like a fly. The Molokan marched toward her, then reached down and choked her. She squirmed and struggled, but no matter what she did, she couldn't escape the vise of his grip.

Her vision began to fade. Her essence was slipping away, as if the Molokan were consuming it. In utter exhaustion, she stopped her writhing. And in one last gasp, she summoned the dragon.

And the dragon came.

When its four immense legs touched down, the earth quaked. The volume of small arms fire intensified as the soldiers unloaded their rifles at a target that was now much easier to hit.

The dragon stomped toward the Molokan, flattening Bolsheviks in its wake. A well-aimed tank round slammed into the dragon's hide, blunting its advance ever so slightly.

Distracted, the Molokan backed away from Yulia. He organized his forces into a coordinated defense.

"Aim for the heads," he shouted.

Yulia stumbled to her feet. Searching for the remaining five psychics, she identified them for the dragon. One brawny male psychic stood on the back of a T-34, directing fire against the wyrm. The dragon crushed him and the tank under its enormous forepaw. A blonde woman huddled behind an oak tree as she launched psychic attacks against the dragon. Within seconds, the dragon rendered her and the oak into a smoldering ash heap.

The surviving T-34s systematically directed their fire at a single head. In a riot of smoke and flames, one of the dragon's necks collapsed. Three men armed with flamethrowers rushed to the scene, cauterizing the headless stump.

The area was like the surface of a volcano with smoke and pyres of flame erupting everywhere. But the dragon's efforts were flagging. Yulia had to do something, so she used the chaos to her advantage. She made Gordunov believe the three remaining psychics were Nazis.

Gordunov marched toward his first victim and gutted her with his bayonet, his faced twisting in a snarling rictus. Then he gripped her male companion by the neck and crushed the man's windpipe.

The last surviving psychic, the woman the Molokan had called Anastasiya, shifted her attention to Gordunov. Half a heartbeat later, his head exploded in a scarlet mist. But half a heartbeat was all Yulia needed. Reaching into Anastasiya's mind, Yulia absorbed the woman's deepest fears and turned them against her. Anastasiya spent her final moments tearing her face off to remove phantom spiders.

Now Yulia sought out the Molokan. More confident in her powers, she yearned to make him suffer. But the dragon's sorry state gave her pause. Two of its necks lay smoldering on the ground, their stumps cauterized. Its third head fought for its life with fire, fang, and fury.

Another tank round slammed into its snout. Yulia couldn't afford the luxury of chasing the Molokan now. She had to save the dragon.

Yulia set her sights on a T-34. Seconds later, its turret slewed toward an adjacent tank. The first tank's commander seemed perplexed and yelled at the gunner inside the cupola. But he was too late. An instant later, the neighboring T-34 was a smoking ruin. A third tank fired at the first, punching a smoking hole into its flank.

The dragon lifted its remaining head and beat its wings in an attempt to escape. Just as it took flight, a tank round severed a wing in a riot of bone and smoke. The dragon collapsed and the ground trembled.

Two more T-34s rolled into position and trained

their main guns on the beast. The dragon sent Yulia an image: an egg perched in the cradling branches of an oak tree. *Good,* she thought. *The Molokan would never be able to place the tree; but she would. She knew exactly where to find it.*

The tanks fired, blasting the dragon's last head into oblivion. A euphoric rush of power surged into Yulia, transforming her into a battery brimming with psychic energy.

Somehow she knew it wouldn't last. She had to use it before it faded. And use it she did.

She overturned tanks with her mind. She bashed fleeing soldiers against their T-34s like flies against windshields. She flattened skulls with nary a thought.

Within minutes, every Bolshevik had either fled or suffered a gruesome death.

Only the Molokan remained.

The shock on his face was obvious. He'd counted on Yulia being telepathic, not telekinetic. But Yulia knew those telekinetic powers would only last until the final embers of life faded from the dragon.

She took no chances.

Coiling her energy like a compressed spring, she unleashed it in one defiant blast. The Molokan pitted his own substantial reservoir of power against hers.

It wasn't enough.

She flung him twenty meters, smashing him against an oak tree. Rather than face her, he staggered to his feet and fled.

Yulia wanted desperately to chase and run down her tormentor, but she was utterly spent. Yet she persisted. But when she tried to pursue him, she collapsed from exhaustion.

She despaired as he escaped into the boundless

fields beyond. But then an idea struck her like a mule kick. She could sense his state of mind: frantic. His thoughts, jumbled and frenetic. His mind concentrated on nothing but survival.

So Yulia showed him what he wanted to see with a touch of something even more enticing—*glory*.

* * *

"Teach me everything you know, Molokan," Stalin said. *"As the greatest psychic of your generation, you're the only one worthy of the honor."*

Stalin had never referred to Colonel Petrov that way before. Perhaps he meant it as a compliment; perhaps he was just toying with his prey. With Stalin, you could never be sure. Either way, Petrov stayed on his knees. He found it incredible that Stalin could ignore such a humiliating defeat.

"Comrade Stalin," said Petrov, *"I would be honored to teach you. What brings you this close to the front?"*

Stalin waved his hand dismissively. "Never mind that. I know you think you've failed here, but I assure you, you have not. We still have the egg, no?"

Petrov wanted to slit his own throat. How would he tell Stalin the egg was lost? "Forgive me, Comrade Stalin, but the egg is gone. The great wyrm has hidden it."

"Nonsense. I have agents throughout the Ukraine. I know exactly where it is. All we need do is acquire and protect it."

"But, Comrade Stalin, I thought we were going to use Rasputin's spell to extract the egg's power?"

Stalin paused. He seemed uncertain, but then he waved his hand. "Never mind that. For now, I wish to protect the egg."

"But, Comrade Stalin..."

"*Don't interrupt me. I've made up my mind. I've decided. Now on to more important things. Show me how to master the power of telepathy. I wish to learn how to project an illusion…indefinitely.*"

Marcas McClellan

Mom's Bombs

MOM'S BOMBS WERE NIFTIER than Oppenheimer's. At least, I thought so at the time. Robert was her professor, after all, at Berkeley. When he saw she had an intuitive grasp of his quantum electrodynamics work, he brought her on board the Manhattan Project.

Pops tagged along with her for the better part of the first summer because he had a grant for an archeological dig on a nearby mesa. That only lasted a short while before Pops decided he had to do his part for the war effort and joined the Marines. Last I heard of him was that he was off fighting the Japs somewhere, island-hopping in the South Pacific.

I was seventeen but Mom wouldn't sign the enlistment papers so I could go in early. "One man from this family is enough," she said. "I need you here with me." We fought a lot about that.

After Robert exploded his first bomb in 1945, Mom

made ready to test their *other* bomb, the one *she* designed, the one she called her *causality bomb.* Robert and she agreed that it would be spectacular, but neither of them knew in what way.

As it happened, I was the one that found out what Mom's bombs did.

*   *   *

We were on our way back from Alamogordo to Los Alamos after the atomic bomb blast. I was quiet, in the front seat with our driver, an Apache named Joe, listening, while Robert talked excitedly with Mom in the back seat of the car. "If we can't convince the Japanese with the atomic bombs, we'll have to push forward with *your* project Margaret," he said.

"The ray-gun isn't going to work, Robert," Mom replied. "There's still the five second recharge lag time."

"But the ray-gun *did* work," Robert said. "The science is proven. We just need to change the delivery system."

I was following along pretty well at this point. I'd seen the ray-gun in action, mounted on the back of a Jeep in a 50-caliber mount. The gun itself was about the same size as a 50-caliber machine gun and looked like something out of the lab in the Frankenstein movie. I knew the ray-gun ran off an additional high-power generator off the Jeep's fan belt.

They shot a bunny in a cage. Mom pulled the trigger. A burst of light, without heat, like a lightning bolt. The bunny keeled over from its sitting position, dead, a carrot top still in its mouth.

"We don't even know *what* killed the rabbit!" Mom continued, now upset with what she'd done. "We might cause an *event!*"

My grasp of their esoteric science slipped. I knew

that an event was to be avoided at all costs, but as just what that might be, I was clueless.

Mom continued. "So, you still think we should weaponize it with the grenades and capacitors?" Another of Mom's ideas.

Robert nodded. "It's a sound concept. Pre-charged capacitors from automobile distributors, grenade housings, the *special matter,* proximity fuses—say fifty feet above ground, no, make it twenty-five feet." He leaned into her. I respected the man for his smarts, hated him for taking advantage of Mom's loneliness.

Mom *smiled* at him instead of pushing him away. He lit one of his ever-present cigarettes, offered it to Mom, who shared it with him. "How soon will they be ready, Robert?"

He returned the smile. "Already are. They're on-board a B-25 for a test run tomorrow."

I must have stiffened in my seat. Joe turned to me. His facial features were chiseled in that way that made his age difficult to assess. The lines in his face spoke of innumerable sorrows. We shared a moment before he grinned, the last thing I would've thought his face capable of, then he turned his attention back to his driving.

* * *

Mom and I had our same fight again when we got home. I wanted to do my part, maybe even join up with Pops somewhere on his island-hopping campaign. Mom desperately wanted to keep me safe. My face stung, like I'd put Pop's aftershave on my tender teenage face after shaving, courtesy of the hard slap Mom gave me a few minutes before. I'd accused her of sleeping with Oppenheimer.

Finally, I left the kitchen table, gathered up my camping and dig gear, and slammed the screen door of our house. I wore Pop's mackinaw tied around my waist, sweating as I grunted my way up the steep path. The trail up to Pop's dig site on the next mesa was well-lit by the full moon, but not lit well enough to see all the rattlesnakes that cruised the night, hoping for a mousy meal; so I lit the lantern.

Lit just in time, because there was one on the trail just up ahead. I carefully stepped around it as it rattled, while keeping my eyes open for others that might be in the sagebrush.

At the dig site I considered setting up the small pup tent I had, but the starry sky was nearly cloudless and the July breezes across the mesa, warm, though I knew it would get cold as the night progressed. I opted for a campfire instead.

Pops and I had stocked the place well with juniper and mesquite branches. It didn't take long to get a nice warm fire going. The burning mesquite reminded me of Pop's and me cooking hot dogs at night, with canned chili, after a long dig during the day. Our last trip together especially.

Pops had been excited, for good reason, as we lay in our sleeping bags on either side of our night campfire. "Folsom points, Tom! Think of it," he grinned at me, his eyes sparkling with his happiness.

"*Stone* points," I said, not so enthralled. I liked the broken flints of the Indian arrowheads we'd found in the surface layers of the digs a lot better

"More than that. *Spear* points. They hunted mastodons and mammoths as well as extinct bison. Maybe even Sabre Tooth Tigers!"

"Really?" I said, now impressed.

"And below these layers. What will we find tomorrow?"

I knew this one. Pops talked about it often enough.

"Clovis points?"

Pops nodded. "Hopefully."

Pops ascribed to the theory that humans had used the mesa, this very site, in fact, for thousands of years as a natural fortification.

Suddenly, a loud roar as two twin-engine bombers flew overhead—B-25 Mitchells, on a training mission. Pops stopped smiling.

We left early the next morning instead of continuing the dig.

Hard to believe it had been a year since we last camped together. I thought about what I might find tomorrow. How carefully I would dig around the ancient campfires; the objects I might dig up. I considered my future also. Maybe I'd jump a freight train to Southern California. To Pendleton.

I'd change my name. Lie about my age. I imagined dropping into a foxhole under artillery fire out on the Japanese front lines next to Pops and casually asking him how he was faring.

Yeah, pretty stupid, looking back on it. I fell asleep feeling like a hero.

* * *

Woke, feeling like a fool.

Noise of airplane engines, perhaps the same B-25s that Pops and I had seen a year ago, bearing down on my mesa, close enough to see the bomb bay doors already open.

I skinned out of my sleeping bag dressed only in my skivvies. Stood up, waved my arms, shouted,

"No...no...no...no!"

The first bombs fell short of the mesa. Drifting slowly. Little hand grenade packages suspended by parachutes. As they neared the ground, a brief bright flash, like a miniature lightning strike. Dozens, then hundreds.

I backed up to the edge of the mesa. Behind me a fall of over two hundred feet onto rocks. Not a survivable option. Before me, a hailstorm of Mom's bombs. Not a survivable option either.

I closed my eyes, but still saw the flash through my eyelids.

* * *

"*¡Tengo demonio!*" the Spaniard screamed as he beat on the breastplate of his light armor with his fists, trying to beat *me* out of him.

"*I have a demon!*" I translated quickly. I only had a little Spanish at the time but understood this much. For such a big guy he had a remarkably high-pitched voice.

I was *inside* of this guy, could smell that he hadn't taken any kind of a bath for weeks that competed with his rotten-teeth breath.

Maybe I should've thought about my next actions but acted instinctively. I couldn't read his thoughts, only feel his emotions. I could, however, take over his vocal cords and did. "You don't have a demon," I shouted in English. My voice, surprised both of us because it came out in a gravelly bass. And reaffirmed to the Spaniard that, yes, he was packing a demon.

The man screeched.

"Miguel has no English."

That, from an old Indian man, sitting astride a painted pony, an arrow nocked casually in a magnificent sheep-horn bow. Two other riders, much younger, sat in the same pose astride their war ponies, their bows of a plain wood, probably cedar or mulberry. Pop's archeologist schooling kicking in.

Now, I had the chance to gaze about me and recognize the rock formations and vistas that told me that I was still where I'd bedded down the night before, or was last night in the future now? In any case, if I was still in the same space, but only removed in time, the riders would have to be Apaches.

The old man regarded Miguel suspiciously.

"No...no...no!" This from Miguel. He fell over backwards tangled in his musket trying to remove the carry strap from his shoulder.

The Apaches watched him.

I noticed none of them used their reins—but rather steered with their thighs as they approached, reins draped over their mount's necks—keeping their hands on their weapons.

Miguel had untangled himself from his musket strap and frantically poured powder into its flash pan from a silvered powder horn.

I got a closer look at his musket. I'd seen one like it in a museum. A Model 1803 Spanish Colonial Flintlock Musket. It looked fairly new and gave me a reference point for *when* I might be. Napoleon would have just sold this land to the United States. New Mexico was held by Spanish settlers and ranchers who were taking the land from the native tribes.

"Don't do it!" I shouted again at Miguel as he raised his musket.

Suspicion changed to resolve in the old man's face as he and the two younger riders drew and shot their bows simultaneously.

I felt all of it. The two arrows from the wooden bows slamming into the armor and shallowly penetrating Miguel's chest. It hurt.

But that was nothing compared to getting slammed by the arrow from the old man's sheep-horn bow. The arrow punched through the armor, into Miguel's gut, and into his spine. Burning fire, then icy cold as I lost sensation below the waist.

It took my breath away.

I smelled the shit from oozing bowels and from his wet, pissy, shitty breeches as Miguel's bowels and bladder loosed.

The riders swung their legs casually over their mount's necks and slid to the ground. Walked over. Sat their bows aside. Drew wicked Bowie knives.

*Aha...*Pop's history lessons again incongruously popped into my mind. Bowie knives started being made sometime around the 1820s–1830s.

Miguel's scalp, nose, and ears were the first to go. Then the digits on his hands and feet. He screamed a lot. Each cut, searing, jarring, turning into a dull throb when new cuts happened.

The tongue went next to make room. Yeah, for the whole funky package. We gagged on it.

The three Apaches squatted on their haunches and watched us die.

For some reason, when Miguel's spirit and mine flew his body, we were tangled up together like gum stuck to the bottom of a shoe. We finally tore apart, both of us struggling to make that happen. Miguel ascended...I hoped to a better place. I started to descend...

"No, no, no...not the bad place," my voice wasn't audible, yet the old man's head jerked up, like he heard

me. I turned my attention to him and stopped descending. Started moving toward him. Became one with him. He gasped, fell back.

"A Skinwalker!" he said aloud in English.

"No! No!" I said, this time my voice the high-pitched one. Skinwalkers were evil witches in Navajo culture. I wasn't sure what the Apaches thought of them, other than the old man was aware of them. I knew that the Navajo didn't like talking about them with outsiders so I assumed that the Apache didn't want to either.

"What are you then?"

"A young man; the age of this one."

I raised the arm of the old man, pointed it at the younger of the two other men. He jumped like a rattlesnake had just struck under him. That didn't do anything to reassure the old man either. "Stop that!" the old man said.

"I'm sorry," I said. "This *just* happened to me and I don't know what it is either."

"Where are you from?" the old man said.

"From here, but..." I hesitated. How could I explain that I was from the future?

"But?"

I tried a desperate question. "What year is it?"

"Ah...the Spanish are always saying that it is 1836 of the Year of Our Lord."

That worked. "Then I am from..." I thought quickly. "Then I am from the Year of Our Lord 1945."

The three looked at one another; the younger ones spit out a rapid string in their own language. It didn't sound friendly.

After a bit, the old man shook his head, held up his hand, and they stopped. "My Grandsons think you are an evil spirit and a liar."

Grandsons? I revised my estimate of the old man's age. I had him as possibly the Father or Uncle to these two.

"I do not lie. Do you think I feel like I'm lying to you from inside right now?"

The old man considered for a while before nodding. "You speak truth, though I don't understand how it can be so."

"I don't understand how it happened, either," I said.

The old man nodded again. "Again, I *feel* you speak truth. Perhaps tell us what you *do* know."

I started telling him about a future war with a people far from these lands—even about how his descendants would be fighting the enemy alongside my people. His Grandsons looked skeptical. We crouched together on our haunches and his Grandsons finally nodded along to the story.

"These Jap-neezy—they are evil?" the old man asked.

I shook our head. "Not all. Some are good people, I'm sure. War brings out the worst in people, I think."

"This is so." He turned to his Grandsons and they conversed for a few minutes.

The older Grandson walked over to his pony and reached his hand into a beaded buckskin saddle bag, pulled out a live armadillo by the tail, brought it back kicking and twisting.

"We were going to eat this if we did not catch Miguel today," the old man said. "You may have it."

"Have it?" I said.

"To live inside of while we return to my village and talk about whether we will help you."

"Wait...*help* me?"

"I think it is only *time* that is your enemy now, for many years to come." I felt his smile. "You might want to share those years *with* us if we decide to allow it."

I felt incredibly lonely all of a sudden. I decided to answer diplomatically. "Thank you for considering this."

The old man held up his hand again. "I do not say that we *will* do this thing. Many will say that you can only be evil coming from Miguel."

"What's Miguel's story?" I said.

"He raped and killed my Granddaughter," the old man said.

I didn't ask anything more about Miguel. Instead, "Your English is very good," I said. "Where did you learn it?"

"We trade with white man fur trappers. Learn from them." We got that far before the old man decided that they really had to go, and would I please leave him and go into the armadillo?

I wasn't sure how to go about it at first. It felt a bit like straining when sitting on a toilet. The old man grunted out funny sounds, but we finally managed to pull it off.

I possessed the armadillo. It didn't like it much, hissing at my presence as it scurried away. It'd be easier next time.

They mounted up and didn't return for some days.

*   *   *

The armadillo froze in place at the shrill screech of a hawk above it. A minute later, when the screech echoed from further away, it returned to munching the maggots writhing in the eye sockets of the dead Spaniard.

A rattle of sound, hoofs striking stone and the bray of a mule.

The armadillo lifted its head and sniffed at the surrounding air. It sat back on its hind legs, lifting its head toward the light breeze that drifted across the top of the mesa. Its vision was poor but its hearing and sense of smell excellent.

There, more of the two-legged ones, leading pack mules. Headed toward it, their shiny armor helmets reflecting the hot New Mexico sun. The armadillo sighed, loathe to move away from the maggot bonanza, but I sensed its fear as it jumped down from the soldier's breastplate, and waddled away before it could be seen and killed by the predators.

I chose to be a hobo on the armadillo train today. I had a lot on my mind and wondered what had happened to my body up on the mesa. Mom surely would have gone crazy and went there by now; or maybe not. Did my time there and here follow linearly?

After all, from where I now lived, my death on the mesa hadn't even happened yet. It gave me a headache trying to figure it all out. I even wondered if there was now a spirit bunny from Mom's ray-gun blast wandering around the area inside of a cougar or something else.

Meanwhile, I now camped inside an armadillo slumbering in its burrow.

The next day it wasn't the Grandfather who finally returned to Miguel's death site, to greet me in my armadillo self, but rather his younger Grandson who dismounted his pony and crouched down before me, pointing at his chest.

I dug in the back feet of the armadillo while my ride scurried its front feet as fast as it could, dragging our scaly ass around in circles, trying to escape.

"Tarak," he said, slapping his chest. I found out later the name meant 'Star'.

He then pointed at me, pointed at himself, then clenched his hands together like he was celebrating a win at a baseball game as a pitcher or something.

Okay, he wants me to join him. It was easier to leave this time.

Tarak barely noticed when I slipped inside him, instead lunging forward and grabbing the tail of the little armadillo before it could scurry away. He swung it hard against a rock outcrop one time—very efficient, that, and then settled down to build a fire to cook it.

I watched, interested.

He piled up some dry grasses, removed a couple of stones from a little buckskin pouch he carried on his belt, struck them together. Sparks flew...a few seconds later he leaned over it and blew softly, adding more material as the little wisp of smoke turned into flame. His movements were so economical I could tell that he'd done this many, many times. He said nothing.

I was okay with that.

He pulled out his Bowie knife. I knew where it had been so this part was a bit harder to watch. He spoke then, sort of a mumble. I suspected that he was thanking the Creator or apologizing to the armadillo or something, or maybe even thanking it for providing us food. Once Tarak and I developed enough language between us to communicate, I understood that it was a bit of all of the above. But that was several days away. His English wasn't quite as good as his Grandfather's.

The seared meat was delicious. I could taste it through Tarak's taste buds. Yeah, pretty porky. And I tried not to think about what it had been feeding on.

Tarak and I spent several days taking turns

pointing at things and sounding them out to each other as we travelled on his pony away from the mesa. A few days later I was able to ask him the question that had been on my mind.

"Where is your Grandfather?"

I felt Tarak's frown, then his mimic of sticking his tongue out and holding a rope suspended over his head.

"Hanged?"

Tarak nodded. "Yes, Spaniards hanged Grandfather."

"Because of Miguel?"

Another nod.

It's not like I expected justice for them. I knew enough history to know that they'd already been screwed over by Europeans for centuries and I knew that the worst was still to come for the Apache.

Shortly after that, we entered forested upcountry on his pony; in the mountains north of the Taos Pueblo. It was colder now; we were well into September and the Aspens had turned golden. Snow fell onto the higher peaks at night and melted during the day. I worried about Tarak. And I wondered more about what had occurred to make him decide to host me. "What happened after you and your brother and Grandfather returned to your village?"

"They hanged Grandfather and my brother, Itzachu. I was out hunting, or they would've hanged me too. Now, I must stay away."

"Ah, I'm sorry."

"It is what is." I felt his smile. "Now, *we* are friends and brothers?"

"Uh, yes!" I spoke with spontaneous feeling.

"This is good. Now show me again how to shoot a deer."

I grinned, dismounted, and nocked an arrow to the

bowstring.

We'd been practicing. Tarak shot a bow the same way he did everything—for him, his outdoor skills were as natural as breathing. There was enough muscle memory from Tarak that if I quickly nocked an arrow and shot before I thought about it, I hit what I wanted to every time. This was different. I wanted to do it for myself.

My own arrows landed mostly in the ground around the tree. A few stuck in the tree above the bark. The closest was about a foot away above the bark, stuck in the tree.

"Pah, it does not come by wishing. I spent many, *many* times *trying* to do before I do."

I felt Tarak relax again, to withdraw from the process as much as he could, as I gripped the bow in my hand. We'd set up a small piece of bark atop a short log. It was a good distance, maybe fifty yards. The height, roughly corresponded to a deer's chest, where the heart and lungs were. You couldn't just sight along the arrow. You needed to raise the aim point slightly because the arrow dropped at that distance. Again, I didn't just snap-shoot. I wanted it to be *me* that learned this skill.

"Remember that your eye sees where the arrow goes."

I nodded, pulled. Shot. Split the bark. We both whooped.

Tarak took control, whooping and dancing. I joined him in spirit, now two young teenagers celebrating life.

Tarak stopped suddenly, lifted his head. I could feel his resolve. "We need a woman!"

"*What?*"

"We need to celebrate this."

"I, uh..."

"You've been with a woman before, yes?"

"Well, uh..." I thought to lie, but he'd know. "Um, no."

"Then we *definitely* need a woman. I know one."

*   *   *

And so, it was later that I found myself relaxing in the arms of Doña, a young Spanish woman that Tarak knew, on a raised brush and grass bed covered by cattle robes and smelling of sage. It was too hot to sleep beneath the tattered old Navajo blanket near the fire.

The experience had been all that Tarak promised on our ride back to his village. I'd listened while he boasted and lied about his sexual conquests as we picked our way on his pony through the Aspens on our trip down to lower elevations.

Yes, I knew when he lied.

It's hard to hide when you are so close, but I didn't call him on it. I was comfortable with just being myself and respecting Tarak just being Tarak. Tarak hadn't just rode into the village. Instead he'd tied up his pony well away from it and waited until darkness to sneak into Doña's wickiup. That made me think that perhaps Tarak had enemies in his band that might turn him over to the Spanish for a reward. As much as Tarak had a young man's needs, I felt this gesture had been more for me than him. I couldn't allow him to so endanger himself for me in the future.

Doña and Tarak slept. I didn't. Actually, I didn't sleep at all now, courtesy of the *event*. It gave me lots of time to think about things.

I also started thinking about the long years ahead of us. Over one hundred of them.

If my *event* spirit didn't diminish over time, and I was able to live through all those years, it meant I wouldn't always be with Tarak. He would die, sooner or later. There would have to be others.

I could get by in animals maybe for a time, but the companionship with Tarak had already shown me how much nicer it was to have a human and a friend. Tarak must have felt me worrying because he woke, disentangled us from Doña's arms and slipped out of bed. He picked up his clothes and we went outside before he dressed. I waited quietly. I didn't trust the others in the wickiups around us, not knowing who our enemies were. We slipped from the village, walked back to his tethered pony before he spoke. "It won't be easy,"

"That's why I was restless—thinking that very thing."

"I felt that. But you don't have to do it alone... unless you don't want to be with me?" he said with a twinge of anxiety.

"Ridiculous. Of course, I want to be with you."

I felt Tarak's smile. "This is good."

We spoke no more for the rest of the night, content to let the pony find its own way through the darkness, away from the village.

* * *

I would have died that first winter if I'd been on my own.

Liluye—'Hawk Singing' was the name Tarak gave our daughter. She was born in the Summer before the rains. During a lightning storm.

Tarak and I weren't there for the birth, but nearby. The Spaniards still hunted us.

Unfortunately, Tarak, his wife, and daughter

succumbed to tuberculosis before New Mexico became a territory.

I grieved for a long time and left to mourn alone; lived with birds for a time, finally settling on owls and hawks since it was less disrupting for me to be the predator than the prey.

The harder years came for the Apaches, then passed. Tarak's band finally got their Reservation in 1887.

Joe was born in 1901. I didn't realize it at the time, but I'd been watching his ancestors while I lived in my various guises.

Coyotes, a deer, once—the deer really *hated* being around the two-leggeds that hunted them—hawks, owls, armadillos, skunks, weasels, even dogs and cats. Different shells to pass the time in.

I was a cat when I met Crazy Cat Woman for the first time. That was her name and she really was crazy. She trapped and ate cats, and on the day I met her, the cat was *me*. Not your normal crazy cat lady. Being crazy as she was, I wasn't sure she would even notice when I joined her. But when I leapt over, she smiled and started dancing, ululating words I could only guess at.

"About time, Spirit Walker."

"Wait, you know 'bout me?"

"Shouldn't I? You've been in and out of animals and us for some time. There's *stories* about you."

I really didn't want to know about those, so I didn't ask.

We put on our cat-fur robe of many hues and mews one day to prepare for a visit to her niece, her talking to her 'friends' all the time, the cats that wound themselves around her feet in her wickiup and the voices that spoke to her in her head. Even the deceased cats in her robe.

I couldn't hear the others she heard, but she had a name for each and every one of us.

"Yes, yes, little white man. We will ask if the baby's name is Joe if it is a boy," she said to my question. She sat down on her sage bed and pulled her moccasins on. They were an interesting construction. Sturdy elk hide for the soles, and cat-fur leggings. Attached to the moccasins, a cat's head and tail on each.

"You ready?" she said. I couldn't tell if she was talking to me or the shoes. "After that, shall we catch us a cat for the pot?" She stood up and shuffled forward, her cat-headed footwear nodding back to her in agreement.

Let's just say I brought a little normality to her life and leave it at that.

The others treated her with great respect, her being spirit-touched. She also knew a lot about herbal medicines and was the first one called if a birth was difficult.

Crazy Cat Woman's niece said her baby's name was Joe. But I waited until he was a teenager to introduce myself to him, when I could see the resemblance to his older self.

At first, he thought he'd caught the crazy from his aged Aunt. But it didn't take long for me to convince him that he was to play a special role. When the United States entered the war in 1917 and he wanted to lie about his age and enlist, I didn't try to stop him.

We fought in the trenches 'over there' and came back home. When the other doughboys mustered out, I convinced him to stay in, and we moved around within the state, working at the different Army installations.

He married and fathered children. I didn't allow

myself to get close to any of them this time. Finally, he started driving for Dr. Oppenheimer.

"When do you go back to yourself?" Joe asked me one day. We were watching Pops and my teenage self, climbing the trail to our dig site on the mesa next to the Los Alamos installation.

"About a year," I replied.

"Good," he said.

* * *

Joe and I watched Mom and Oppenheimer asleep in the back seat of the car through the rearview mirror. It wouldn't be long now.

I'd had many years to rehearse what I was going to tell them. Why they mustn't proceed with Mom's bombs. How the last thing we wanted was hundreds of angry disembodied Japanese waiting for the opportunity to exact their vengeance. My story would be long and filled with enough detail to convince them, I was sure. And then there was Joe. I'd seen him in action when he charged into the Huns. No, Mom and Oppenheimer would come around or else. Joe and I had put jerry cans of gasoline in the trunk of the car and were willing to do whatever it took to keep Oppenheimer and Mom from green lighting her bombs. A fiery crash in the desert, if they didn't heed us.

I heard Mom yawning. Oppenheimer lit up a cigarette. They'd start talking about the bombs soon. I meant to interrupt them.

Joe and I turned to my teenage self and *grinned* before I jumped over.

Ron Wolfe

The Road of a Thousand Wonders

THE CONDUCTOR CALLED, "NORTH PLATTE," and Caleb felt a thud in his heart as if the train had jolted. Standing, he nearly fell.

"North Platte, Nebraska."

The steam whistle blasted over the conductor's announcement of the date, the all-important date of arrival, but still—

It was the right place, and it could be the right time, this time. His time! Now!

But he wasn't positioned, seated, to leave the train, and what if the chance never came again? He didn't know all the rules, or who made the rules, but he knew the one that came with the ticket: no promises.

The train slowed into the station. Westbound from out of the night, out of the stars, into the lights of the train yard. Bailey Yard. The Union Pacific hub brought trains from everywhere to the middle of nowhere, this small town surrounded by sand-hills and corn fields.

Caleb tried to translate the blur of red and green signal lights into his memory of this same place as it had looked once a time ago, on a day as blue as the light off a gun barrel. But the the dark held tight to its mysteries.

He had seen the yard just that one time, witnessed through the eyes of just another Army draftee on his way east—thinking there was nothing that could hurt worse than the hopeless void inside him, no idea how a bullet felt.

Eastbound Caleb Brennan: never "Mr. Brennan," never "Cal," sometimes called "Red" as much for the tinge of his ears as for the spill of red hair that was one of the first things the Army took away from him. He was a freckle-faced stretch of arms and legs, and icy shards of nerves and loneliness on his first-ever train ride. Eastbound to Piedmont, N.Y., to ship out from the Hudson River port to—destination? Not for him to know.

He was 18 years of not-quite-manhood, the whole of him compressed to smaller than life in a stiff uniform. The train had arrived in a hoot-and-holler, steam and blue sky, the jostling excitement that came with a load of soldiers and the prospect of 15 minutes' freedom. North Platte's Front Street offered the speediest brothels this side of Omaha.

Caleb had moved only to gain a window seat on that sleeted morning in February, 1941, and then not to look out at the train station. He breathed against the glass to make a circle of condensation, in which he could pretend to see the white siding of the farm home he had left a thousand miles behind. The sugar beet acres, and his dad left alone to do the work of a younger man.

But the fog cleared to a very different sight, a different kind of warmth, and just a pane of glass away. And ever since, he had tried to imagine her name. Sheila. Jeanette. Margie, Margie, Margie.

Margie of the green-green eyes.

* * *

Westbound Caleb Brennan fingered the wet cardboard ticket out of his olive drab shirt pocket, and verified how the front of the ticket read through the red blotches: "North Platte, Nebraska. December 22, 1944."

He tried again to make out the "Riders' Rights and Responsibilities" on the back, but only the first lines remained legible as the meaning extinguished into smaller and smaller print.

Caleb searched his fellow riders for any sign that one of the seated might be ready to leave the train. If any of the seated got up, then he, Caleb, could take that spot. The ticket was clear on that much: He would gain the rights of a seated passenger.

"This your stop, son?"

"Could be," Caleb said with a nod that his long neck overstated. He looked for the man who had spoken to him, for the source of this tired voice in the tremble of mist that surrounded him, that filled the aisle.

"Ever done this before?" the man said, closer but no more distinct. "No? I didn't think so. You look like I felt the first time I jumped out of a transport. Five–Eleventh Parachute Infantry. Got a cigarette?"

Caleb found the pack, tapped out a Lucky Strike

for a fellow soldier.

The man sparked a Zippo lighter that brought his facial planes into focus for a flickering moment. Flat nose. Partial smile. Partial blank.

"Mine's Laramie, Wyoming, not here," the man said. "I don't mind letting go a couple pointers. How to watch these people. I know enough, I've come close to a seat more than once."

Caleb felt hands on his shoulders from behind, a touch that melted through him as the almost imaginary pressure urged him closer to the seated passengers.

"You can't wait for somebody to get up," the man said. "By that time, you're too late. Somebody else'll have the seat. Miss your chance, you're done—you'll candle out. Way to do this, you watch all the little ways they move. See—that one across, she's got her shoulder angled toward the aisle. She's likely. And that one, the finger drum on the arm rest, but he hasn't once glanced out. He's impatient. He wants to keep going, doesn't want the train to stop. I'd fix on that woman three up, see? The strawberry that straightened her hat. Try to work your way that direction. Be ready to move fast."

Caleb did try, but the air seemed to thicken around him. Dense. Hard to move, impossible to see through. He pressed, but the standing opposed him. They blocked him with smeared impressions of bodies crushed together, currents of cold and colder, a hand in his face, a fist thrown.

He was just behind the strawberry blonde with the green-ribboned hat, the perfect curl of hair at the back of her neck. Familiar, so familiar.

The train slowed to a meditative clack-clack, broken by a second long blast from the locomotive's steam trumpet, the hiss of the air brakes.

She stood, half-stepped into the aisle. Caleb plunged for the empty seat. In the blur and collision that forced him aside, he came so close to her that he physically brushed her shoulder. The touch left a here-and-gone blood stain on her crisp white sleeve. She turned to him with eyes the green of a satin ribbon —the green that melted winter.

"Do I know you?" she asked, and he would have said yes—yes!—don't you see?—and you've known me forever, Margie!—but the green eyes lost focus, and the face sank to confusion, and she turned as if she hadn't seen him at all.

What ever made him expect more? He'd been nothing more than a passing uniform to her, a glance through the train window, and he'd clung to her smile like a photo of a movie star, folded and kept safe under the band in his helmet.

The conductor's last call broke the spell.

"North Platte," the big man hailed. He strode the aisle is if it were empty. The brass plate on his blue cap made the conductor and his pronouncement official: "North Platte. June 11, 1953," and she was gone.

Out the window this time, Caleb saw her meet a red-headed soldier on the platform, caught a glimpse of the small drama—the lucky man's slow step toward her. Hers toward him. The embrace—was it?—that was blanked from Caleb's view by a flash of sunlight on glass.

* * *

The locomotive cried its departure, two longs. The brakes released, and the train pulled forward, built speed through the smoke and steam that clouded the windows. Caleb saw the contested seat was occupied by a crew-cut young serviceman like him, only the uniform was different—a Marine.

The winner allowed himself only a moment's expression of relief as he settled in, and then leaned forward as if to make the train run faster, hands clasped in a white knot between his knees.

"Ever wonder where other people are going?" The raspy-voiced woman spoke at Caleb's side. "Why it's so important for them to be there?"

Caleb straightened, weak with failure. Train in motion, the haze thinned in a barely-felt breeze, a swirling wreath around her thin face.

"I have my reasons," she said, "and what do you care?"

"Enough," Caleb said.

"Oakland, California," she said, looking down to the thrumming floor as if Oakland might appear at her feet, her lace-up ankle boots, Old Mother Hubbard's farm work footwear. "I have a son there."

Caleb wanted to look away away from the vapor shape of her, to look back in the solid direction of North Platte.

"He doesn't know I'm coming," she said, "but I have to know. Night my husband left, he told my son why. He never told me, and I have to know why. My boy, he had his father's cold eyes, and he showed me his father's Buck knife. Never had a knife before. I didn't cry the morning the boy lit out, too, dared me to stop him. I saw him off from the gate. I thought, well, mister, there you go. There you go, Thad, my honey boy, poisoned by whatever he told you, off to be a cruel man of your own, and I wished I'd cut his hair one last time."

The train ran hard and straight away from Caleb's destination.

"Pinkertons found him for me," the woman said. "Cost everything I had, but for train fare and burial, and it seems like all for nothing. How much can you see of me? Anything at all of me? I can't see my own hands."

She cocked her phantom head at Caleb like a chicken at a moth, and said, "No need to answer me. What's your story?"

"Don't guess I have one," Caleb said. "But I know one."

He told about the nobody-from-nowhere on the troop train, newly-drafted and on his way to war. How he sat alone by the window when the train stopped in North Platte on the way east, and how the rap-rap-rap on the frosted glass made him slide the window open. And the green eyes that met his.

"Here," she said, "to let you know somebody cares about you," and she handed the soldier a plate with a cloth napkin over it. "Here—to say thank you, to say be safe, to say come back whole. My name is—"

The train's departure stole her name, but not her face from Caleb's memory. He left the window open, let the ice pellets sting his face, on the chance he might see her again. Another soldier had to close it. Caleb made the sandwich and the chocolate-chip cookie last to Chicago, and he still had the apple in France.

* * *

Caleb watched the windows to see the world change from bright to dusk, twilight to floating through stars. Wagon trains and stagecoaches had gone this same way, east and west on the Overland Route from

Omaha, Nebraska, to San Francisco, California. But the train held to no line of time or season. The ride made good on Union Pacific's promised "road of a thousand wonders."

He watched as the train pulled into Ogden, Utah, on Nov. 15, 1955, in a blanketing snow that obscured the station. An old man in a notched-brim cowboy hat stepped off, one hand gripping the collar of his flannel jacket against the cold, the other cradling a rose-patterned, round box tied with thick red yarn. The old hand stood alone, waiting as if for someone to meet him on the platform. The storm faded him to a snow-ghost, and blew him to powder as the train moved on.

A slab of a man in a pin-striped suit got off on a burning blue day in Reno, Nevada, on Aug. 1, 1931. The suit had extra-wide shoulders he didn't need, that gave him the shape of a triangle balanced on a dainty point of gloss-polished black Florsheims. The train pulled away to the snare drum static of one-two-three, a dozen gunshots against the steam whistle.

Each time one of the seated passengers rose to leave the train, the standing made another rush for the empty seat. And each time one of the standing gained a seat, he gained a presence as well, a weight, a reality. This man—a scent of Wildroot Cream Oil hair tonic. This woman—a living color and urgency, a ceaseless tap-tapping of the right foot, a sweat stain on the high lace collar, eyes on the move, a fugitive in hiding.

"Purgatory," she said to the empty air. "Purgatory, or is it hell? Am I out? Am I going home?" But she had taken her place among the living, and the living could not hear the dead.

Something more hopeful than Purgatory, they told her. Something much, much more complicated than hell. Not likely bound for heaven. And where did you buy your ticket, lady? Who sold it to you? Why can't you remember?

*   *   *

"North Platte, you said?" The voice spoke to Caleb the way that comes low from a heavy build, a man's voice with the bellows to be heard above steam and rail. "I'm lucky, I saw the war canteen."

He told about the troop trains that arrived in North Platte at all hours. The eastbound carried recruits. The westbound came back with wounded in the front, coffins in the back cars. The people of North Platte met every train. A few volunteers, and then many organized the North Platte Canteen in the train station. The canteen dispensed coffee and sandwiches, and maybe more—maybe a few minutes' salvation of a kind that came warm and sweet, and sprinkled with war-rationed sugar.

And later, at Normandy and Anzio and Hurtgen Forest, they would remember this stop in a place they'd never heard of before. They would talk, they would dream about North Platte as if only in dreams could such a place exist. They found no shame in weeping over a thought of North Platte. Damn sight rather be in North Platte. North Platte has the prettiest. Going back to North Platte.

Caleb's new traveling companion smelled of spearmint. He tapped out two sticks of Beech-Nut chewing gum, offering the first to Caleb. The rest of the pack went back to the top left pocket of his bib overalls, where the sewn-on patch read, "Steve Levy."

"Been there before?" he said. "I mean been there to set foot?"

Caleb shook his head.

"Know when you have to be there?"

Caleb named the date.

"Thought so. Bastogne, was it? Don't know?"

Caleb didn't.

"I don't expect it matters," the man said. "Ticket tells all you need to know. Could be that everything comes clear to you once you got two feet on the ground, or maybe you go through the rest of eternity as dumb as a beetle. Me, I got no destination, except—"

He jabbed a thumb toward the front of the train.

"I belong up there," he said, "and there's no way to get through the cars from here to there—I know, I've tried—so I ride like I don't know any better."

He tugged at the fingers of his yellow gloves, the fingers blackened and the cuffs speckled with cinder burns.

"Fifteen years, I worked my up brakeman to engineer," he said. "Seventeen years an engineer, Sonny Jim, and let me tell you there's no where else to be, not once you've been up there. Up there's my North Platte. It's a sweet smooth ride back here. Up there, you ride the fire dragon, and she throws you side to side, but she knows you've got the hand on her."

* * *

Julesburg, Colorado. May 12, 1913. A mother and baby left the train. Caleb liked to think someone had given her a seat. He wondered if he would have made the sacrifice. He didn't like the answer.

Winnemucca, Nevada. Sept. 20, 1961. He came so close to seated, just for a moment, he could feel the soft red velvet upholstery, the cool touch of the polished brass support, trace the lines in the wood paneling.

Oakland, California. Dec. 3, 1947. He saw the farm woman candle out. Left standing, she could not leave the train. She had missed her stop. Her mouth opened to a silent scream, and closed to a dot of gas-flame blue light, all that was left of her, and the light ebbed away in mid-air. She never would find her son, never solve the mystery of her family's tragedy, never know the consequence of asking.

* * *

"North Platte. April 14, 1896," the engineer said. "It was only a whistle stop that day, but such a commotion —I mean horses and horse gear, and cowboys, I saw Indians—even had a bright red stagecoach, and all this being loaded on rail cars."

The excitement made him chew his gum faster, flavoring the scene this time with kissing-sweet chlorophyll.

"And there he was in lordly fashion, himself atop the biggest, whitest stallion of the lot. Buffalo Bill Cody, I mean Buffalo Bill and no mistake, the buckskin and the high boots, Buffalo Bill and his Wild West Show. But shut me up, Jim, that's only the second best thing I ever saw in North Platte."

Caleb's legs and feet looked to him as if he were standing waist-high in milky water. He had lost his fingertips. The engineer's face, nearly transparent, showed a blue dot of light between the eyes.

"Not much left of you but the hole in the donut," the engineer said. "Me, I can't even hold an idea, anymore. But this one's important. Tells you something about the good in people. Now, you might hear a hundred versions of this story, but I was right there when it happened. It was a winter night, midnight, one of those war years. Had to stop for maintenance, and my plan was to pay respects to a certain little Susie Q. on Front Street. But I'd heard about the canteen. Got there, and it was a full-swing party, and the girls —how do I say this? The girls were the kind that if they kissed you, which they wouldn't, none of that, but if they did—and this sergeant came in."

He told the version where the sergeant comes in hobbling on a cane, his right shirt sleeve pinned up. The bad leg and the missing arm made him reel to the side. Still and all, if you were twice his size, you wouldn't mess with him. He comes up to the coffee counter, orders two cups.

The sergeant says: *One's for me, one's for my pal. He's not here. But I want you to keep that coffee hot for him. Keep it all the time in that same cup, with the chip on top the handle, 'cause nobody and nothing comes through a war in one piece whole, but we stand up to what we lost.*

This guy, my pal—he wasn't much of a soldier, that's what I thought. But he picked me up, and he carried me one hell of a mile back to the line. He would have made it all the way, but he caught a stitch across the back. Straight through him, straight through my leg. Even then, he went down as slow as he could to his knees. He wouldn't drop me. He said, "I'm sorry, sir. I meant to bring you home."

One's for me, one's for my pal, and I want you to keep that coffee hot for him.

* * *

Caleb got the idea just past Colfax, California, on a bright March morning, 1891. The candy butcher had come through, a waist-high kid, probably a run-away, with his canvas bag of wares that included horehound lozenges and cigars. The cigar stench mingled with the wood pulp-smelling smoke from the stove that burned in the far back corner of the crowded car.

"There's a way to the locomotive," he told the engineer. "Try for the next stop. Once you're off the car, then all you have to do is move your feet. Just run and get up there, Mr. Levy. Up where you belong."

"Used to belong," the engineer said. He was blue light more than anything else. "Maybe I don't, anymore."

"Maybe you'll find out this train needs a new engineer."

"I'd grab hold that Johnson Bar one more time. Give 'er two blasts, and ease back on the throttle. Man!"

The conductor called, "Soda Springs. Soda Springs, Idaho, and step lively. Soda Springs, May 19, 1967."

"First thing, you need a seat," Caleb said. "I know enough, I've come close to a seat more than once. What you do, you watch all the little ways they move—"

*   *   *

The conductor called, "North Platte. North Platte, Nebraska."

Caleb tried to pull himself tall as the train slowed. The conductor walked the aisle, through the phantoms. Caleb watched, but no one in the car gave any sign of leaving. The conductor neared, swinging his watch on a gleaming gold chain. He clicked open the watch front, consulted the dial.

"North Platte," the conductor called. Caleb's destination—the name he recalled so clearly printed on the ticket.

"December 22, 1944," the conductor called. Caleb's date—clearly on the ticket, but he couldn't remember who sold him the ticket, or how he paid for it, or what he'd done with it.

Nobody moved, none of the seated passengers. The first sliver of dawn scratched a rose-colored line across the windows. Where the glass might have reflected a man in Caleb's place, it gave back nothing but a glint of blue.

The seated were mostly asleep, jumbled against each other. Each two or three of them, family or strangers, seemed to have voted on whether to topple left or right, and nobody stirred. Nobody would.

The conductor walked directly to Caleb. His eyes came level to Caleb's. His eyes and his uniform were the same shade of cobalt. He smoothed the ends of his mustache. Caleb had known officers less imposing than the conductor, men of rank who looked right through him. Maybe he'd always been a ghost.

"Special arrangements have been made for you, Mr. Brennan," the conductor said, "if you would follow me." He extended a formal arm to point the way. " I have a seat for you. Compliments of the new engineer."

The seat placed Caleb in a separate car with just a few other passengers spaced out. His sense of smell came back with the message that the car reeked of smoke, but his uniform repelled the surroundings, clean and crisp, ready for inspection. His fingers came back with a stiff ache, and his hands with a stinging clap, and a clap-clap together, and his legs with a spring that lifted him with solid weight as the train rolled to a stop.

"Watch your step, sir," the conductor said as Caleb exited the car, one foot and another on the concrete platform. He walked to the sign that read: NORTH PLATTE CANTEEN. He fell in with a crowd of servicemen bounding through the open doors.

The jukebox played *I'll Get By* with Harry James

and His Orchestra, and Bing Crosby's *Swinging on a Star* over a scene that resembled the sweet oven fragrance and commotion of a state fair bake-off. Caleb made his way past tables of cakes and cookies and sandwiches, offered by women in white kitchen aprons. Mothers, grandmothers, sisters, girlfriends, the army of the home front. He returned the smiles of strangers, accepted handshakes, and more and more understood why he was there.

His booted feet led him step-clack across the black-and-white tiled floor to the coffee counter, to the far end of the red-topped counter, to the empty seat and the steaming cup at the far end.

He settled in to drink his coffee with his thumb over the crack on top the handle, and to wait forever, if it takes forever, but maybe no longer than the next arrival, for the green-eyed girl who would step off the train on June 11, 1953.

THIS PAGE LEFT
INTENTIONALLY
BLANK

Curiosities War Dept.

CONTRIBUTORS

JD Blackrose loves all things storytelling and celebrates great writing by posting about it on her website, slipperywords.com. She has published *The Soul Wars* series and the *Monster Hunter Mom* series, both through Falstaff Books, as well as numerous short stories.

No one knows how many of her family were killed because there are none left. One of her grandmother's family, Frances Bader, was rescued as part of Lena's 100. Follow her on Facebook and Twitter.

Adrian Chamberlin is the author of the critically acclaimed supernatural thriller novel *The Caretakers* as well as numerous short stories in a variety of anthologies, mostly historical or futuristic based supernatural horror.

He edited the 2016 supernatural warfare novella collection *Darker Battlefields,* and his novella *The Silent Towers* was shortlisted for Independent Legions Publishing's 2018 Inferno Award. Further information can be found on his website: www.archivesofpain.com

His maternal grandfather, Flight Sergeant Frank Barton, was an aircraft engineer in the RAF and specialised in aviation electronics. He was seconded to the Royal Navy during the war, where he spent a period of time on HMS Orion and then on an unnamed ship in the Caribbean. He never spoke of what he was assigned to do on that placement.

Kevin Frost joined the Navy at 20 after derailing a freshman year. His parents never quite got over it. He was mostly a mechanic, except those three years in Maine which he doesn't talk about much. In retrospect, it was probably less stressful than working for Monsanto.

His grandfather was a radio pioneer in San Francisco who taught the relatively new technology to servicemen shipping out to the Pacific fleet.

Lewis Gershom is a writer of speculative fiction. He writes about issues he sees in his hometown of New York City. His work has appearred in *Metaphorosis, The Nabu Review,* and the anthology *UnrealPolitik* by Jayhenge Publishing in late 2018. When not writing, he teaches middle school English.

While all of his immediate family arrived in the United States before World War II, recently conducted genealogical research shows some of his extended family were killed in concentration camps.

Sean Patrick Hazlett is an Army veteran originally from Wilmington, Delaware, but now makes Northern California his home. His short stories have appeared in *The Year's Best Military and Adventure SF: Volume 4, Year's Best Hardcore Horror Volume 4, Year's Best Hardcore Horror Volume 3, Terraform, Galaxy's Edge, Writers of the Future,* and *Grimdark Magazine,* among others.

His maternal grandfather served as a doctor in the United States Army and his paternal grandfather served on a Liberty ship in the United States Merchant Marine, a service that suffered a larger percentage of war-related deaths than all the other U.S. services with one out of every twenty–six mariners dying in the line of duty.

Andrew J Lucas has contributed to books published by Fasa, Dream Pod Nine, White Wolf Games and Atlas Games among others. His creative output (and enthusiasm) is often blunted by his day job, but he does manage to produce a few projects each year. He has contributed stories to a number of anthologies, but a Google search still won't consistently find his bibliography. He lives in Langley, British Columbia, likes cats, but has none.

His great grandfather was a member of the Queen's lifeguard and was discharged after being buried in an avalanche in France. During the second war his grandfather on his mother's side, an ingenious Scot, taught radio use and served in Bletchley Park, not to outdone his other grandfather was a draftsman designing tanks for Leyland Motors. Needless to say we have a family tradition of giving what for to the Kaiser!

Marcas McClellan lives on the side of an active volcano in Hawaii, so it's understandable why his stories quite often are a bit strange. He is on Facebook alienating half his readers with political rants. Less political on Twitter as @grenitschee.

His father's tombstone reads: KEIGLEY, Kenneth F. 9 Apr 1923-27 May 1969 Ill. Sgt. 427 Night FTR Sq. AAF WWII . His father was a radar operator whose squadron served in Italy, Southern China, Burma, and India in the P-61 Black Widow Night Fighter, the first U.S. aircraft to use radar.

Andrew McCurdy is a writer and editor whose day job as a Speech-Language Pathologist involves helping nonverbal, special needs children access technology to maximize their ability to communicate. He lives in rural Nova Scotia with a twelve-year-old girl, two cats, and a brazen little hamster named Mouse.

Having heard stories, as a child, of family and family-friends surviving prison camps in Germany and Japan, Andrew often imagined elaborate escape schemes, many involving the stealth, speed, and subtlety of that most under-utilized of escape vehicles: the hot-air balloon.

At eighteen, he almost joined the army as a drummer in a marching band until his cousin Bill, with a straight face, convinced him his personality and temperament were better-suited to tree-planting in northern British Columbia. Decades later, reflecting back, his cousin was right.

Mounia Lakehal Meribout was born in Algeria, she is the eldest of five. She works as a Neurologist at a Teaching Hospital, she is married and has two boys. She is a big fan of thrillers. So one day, she thought: "Why not to write one myself?"

Many Algerians fought World War II as legionnaires, as Algeria was a French colony at this time. When the Allies won, a few Algerians manifested their joy in many towns because France promised a glimpse of independence to Algeria. Those manifestations ended with a great disappointment and multiple massacres in the Algerian towns of Setif, Guelma, Kherrata. Since then, May 8th, 1945 is a disastrous date in the history of Algeria.

In other words, Algerians were the victims of the victims in World War II.

Mark Orr lives in Middle Tennessee with his wife of 38 years, a fifteen year old cat named Mehitabel, a history degree and way too many books. On his better days, he gets to play with his grandchildren. His second hard-boiled supernatural mystery novel, *Dead Women in Love,* is being published this summer by Dark Recesses Press. He has recently returned to writing short stories, a form in which he had a small degree of success during the first decade or so of the current millennium.

Mark's grandmother's cousin was a bombardier on a B-17 Flying Fortress that took part in the Schweinfurt-Regensburg raid on August 17, 1943. His crew's mission was to bomb the Messerschmitt factory at Regensburg, but their plane was shot down. He spent the duration of the war in a Luftstalag — a prisoner of war camp for airmen. He weighed ninety pounds when he was liberated. He did not speak kindly of his captors.

Born in Singapore, **Anya Ow** eventually moved to Melbourne to practice law. She now works in advertising. Her short stories have appeared in venues such as *Strange Horizons, Uncanny,* and *Daily SF.*

Her story was inspired by family recollections about surviving the Japanese Occupation. The maternal side of her family hid for part of the war in Malaysia, turning the family estate into a refugee camp to shelter people. Her grandfather helped to fund local resistance. Initially ignored by the Japanese army on their way down to Singapore, the camp was tolerated for a while until resistance fighters killed a senior Japanese officer in another estate, after which it was massacred. The family went on the run, eventually taking shelter in Indonesia.

Anya can be found on twitter @anyasy.

DJ Tyrer is the person behind Atlantean Publishing and has been widely published in anthologies and magazines around the world, such as *Winter's Grasp* (Fantasia Divinity), *Misunderstood* (Wolfsinger), and *Sorcery & Sanctity: A Homage to Arthur*

Machen (Hieroglyphics Press), and issues of *Fantasia Divinity, Broadswords and Blasters,* and *BFS Horizons*.

DJ's great-grandfather was an ARP Warden who was killed in an air-raid and his great-uncles took part in Dunkirk.

https://djtyrer.blogspot.co.uk

Dawn Vogel writes and edits fiction and non-fiction. In her spare time, she also runs a craft business and co-edits *Mad Scientist Journal*. She is a member of SFWA. She lives in Seattle with her husband, author Jeremy Zimmerman, and their herd of cats.

One of her grandfathers served in the Army in Germany as a cook. The other served in the Pacific Theatre, and she treasures his Navy peacoat that her dad and aunt gave her to keep for the family.

Visit her at www.historythatneverwas.com

Suzanne J. Willis is a Melbourne, Australia-based writer, a graduate of Clarion South and an Aurealis Awards finalist. Her stories have appeared in anthologies by PS Publishing, Prime Books, Falstaff Books, and Metaphorosis, and in *Syntax & Salt, Mythic Delirium,* and *Lackington's*.

Her mother, Ann, grew up in outer London during WWII, and Ann's father was a member of the Home Guard.

Suzanne's tales are inspired by fairytales, ghost stories and all things strange, and she can be found online at suzannejwillis.webs.com

Ron Wolfe is a fiction writer, cartoonist and journalist. On newspaper assignment, he rode the Union Pacific's last steam locomotive—an experience that figures into "The Road of a Thousand Wonders." The story is set in his hometown of North Platte, Nebraska, where his grandmother used her war-rationed sugar to make hundreds of birthday cakes for servicemen at the North Platte Canteen. His horror novel, *Old Fears*, (co-written with John Wooley), is optioned for movies and television.

ACKNOWLEDGEMENTS

First off, my sincere apologies to the authors and readers for not getting this issue to press in a timely manner. I am taking the lessons learned from this year and arranging next year's calendar accordingly so everything is done in its proper season.

Much appreciation to the 2019 first readers: Jedburgh Dagger, Serafina Puchkina, Steadman Kondor, and Andrew McCurdy.

Most of the vintage display fonts in this issue came from the Walden Font Company. Thank you for the Black Friday sale. The story typeface is Coldstyle, which was inspired by a 1935 'Old Style' linotype, and gently aged for that mid-century pulp appeal.

On the audio side of the house, a tip of the bowler goes to Kris Law for giving the podcast its signature voice.

A standing ovation to this year's narrators who did strange things in padded closets to bring the stories to life: Elizabeth Chatsworth, Isaiah Plovnick, Alex Ford of Ford Theatre Reunion, Wulf Moon, Sarah Golding, Jim Hodgson, Maria Rose, CB Droege, Bryony CA, and Tabatha Wood; Wilson Fowlie, Alaisdair Stuart, and Matt Dovey from Escape Artists Inc.; and Bookworm Hienrichs, Tepic Harlequin, and Gabrielle Riel from the home team in New Babbage.

Huge kudos to Kevin MacLeod and all the musicians who make their work available for use in independent projects. You make the Internet a nicer place.

To stay up to date on our reading sessions, podcasts, and print and ebook releases, stop by the Curiosities homepage at GalleryCurious.com, or follow us on Twitter @GalleryCurious.

The
little summer that
comes in fall
is the best
season of
them
all